To Dorothy Here's some tall tales from The Canadian North. Enjoy, eh! Margo

What people are saying about P.S. Don't Tell Your Mother

"Margo Bates is one of those rare people with the ability to put the F-U-N in dysfunctional, even if her family history makes me wonder about the wisdom of ringing her doorbell."
Gordon Kirkland, Syndicated Columnist & Entertainer and Author of "When My Mind Wanders It Brings Back Souvenirs"

"A funny and fabulous first book! 'P.S. Don't Tell Your Mother' will make anyone who's lived in or visited a small town laugh out loud. I can't wait for the next one!"
Randene Neill, Anchor, Global Television News British Columbia

"A rollicking good read that serves up a slice of BC's Wild West as tart and sweet and Grandma Mulvaney's lemon meringue."
Sylvia Taylor, Writer, Editor, Instructor and Regional Director, Federation of BC Writers

"Oral history and storytelling doesn't often easily translate into the written word. But Margo Bates has done that with this irreverent account of life in northwestern B.C. in the late 1950s. Told through the eyes of a young girl with the use of letters between her and her grandmother, Bates not only lays out the life of a family back then but provides a social history of the area. That kind of history all too often gets lost as the years move on and Bates has done a valuable service by letting us know how things were."
Rod Link, Publisher/Editor, 'Terrace Standard

P.S. Don't Tell Your Mother

Margo Bates

authorHOUSE™

1663 LIBERTY DRIVE, SUITE 200
BLOOMINGTON, INDIANA 47403
(800) 839-8640
WWW.AUTHORHOUSE.COM

First published by AuthorHouse 10/14/05

ISBN: 1-4208-9075-1 (sc)

Library of Congress Control Number: 2005908988

Printed in the United States of America
Bloomington, Indiana

This book is printed on acid-free paper.

www.margobates.com

P.O. Box 45019, Ocean Park RPO, South Surrey, B.C. V4A 9L1
Telephone: 604-536-9501   Fax: 604-536-9506
E-Mail: margo@margobates.com

Member, Federation of BC Writers and
Erma Bombeck Humor Writers' Group

Contents

Year End Creative Writing Essay by Maggie Mulvaney,
Grade 8, Division B, Skeena Secondary School—Mr. Kenney Powers, Teacher

Acknowledgements

P.S. Don't Tell Your Mother is part fact, part fiction. My grandmother wrote letters to me for over thirty years. So did my Aunt. It was from their chronicles of day-to-day life in Telkwa, B.C. Pop. 852, that I got the idea for this story, and to write in the form of letters.

Though they wrote people nearly every day, neither Nana Noonan nor my Aunt learned to fold a letter. They'd just grab the pile of pages and fold them until the paper fit the envelope.

It made for a reading experience beyond compare. The richness of their descriptions was pure entertainment. What they left out, we read between the lines. Most often they would write about the same thing. Nana wrote to me. My Aunt wrote to my Mom. We could compare the letters and find out the real story. Most times.

All those years sorting out the pages gave me a skill that is one of my best attributes. I am a good organizer, and can read anyone's handwriting, even my Doctor's. It impresses the heck out of my pharmacist.

The incidents and events in this story happened in one way or the other. Some of the physical descriptions of the area are changed for this story, as are some of the dates.

While the characters are based on real people; they are mostly fictional composites. Any relationship to living people is shocking and purely co-incidental.

The Telkwa Barbecue and Smithers Fall Fair are actual events. If you're ever up that way and have the chance, be sure to attend.

The Smithers Skating Club might exist in some form. The Ice Follies is purely fictional. Although there was a skater once …

This book is dedicated to my grandparents, parents, husband, kids and cousins, aunts and uncles, and friends. Thanks for your love, friendship and support. Thanks for the material.

The richness of life in the North Western part of British Columbia is truly something to be celebrated. We're a unique lot. We have a distinct voice.

My husband says, 'You can take the girl out of the north, but you can't take the north out of the girl.' He's right. Who would want to?

These people supported me throughout the writing of *P.S. Don't Tell Your Mother:*

My husband, Russ Froese suggested that I write the stories down. Anyone who knows our family will agree that it is hard to understand us when we try to tell a story and laugh at the same. It's fun to watch, though. Russ also cleverly advised me to include *The Fur Follies* and the recipe for the Telkwa Hall Rum Punch.

My parents Art & Frankie Bates have let me live my life to the fullest, encouraged me to share my experiences, and they taught me to accept others as they are, and treat others as I would like to be treated. Thanks, Mom and Dad. The best gift you've given is the laughter. We do laugh. A lot.

Ana, Rachael, Tommaso, Joel and Perry: I sincerely appreciate your love and friendship. To my mother-in-law Carol, watch for the next book because I will have to add the story about wild boars and waiters named Harry.

To Leanna MacDonald, Rhonda Norbirg, Patsy Kowan, Tammy Charles, Tamara Stanners, and Jackie Davidson: The day-to-day entertainment with you lot smoothed out any tough moments. Thank you for your gifts of friendship and unique senses of humor.

Some of my friends have passed on. They are Susie Meredith, Donna Hollings, "Grandma" Beth Arp, Agnes Johnson, and my father-in-law,

Bernard Fortune. When they were still here, they read excerpts and laughed in the parts that they were supposed to. I cherish their memories.

Both Edie Groening and her granddaughter Stephanie Charles read the early manuscript and offered their opinions, and recommendations. Tamara Stanners, Tuija Seipell, Cheryl Wilson-Stewart, Kelly Stewart, Karen K. Merrell and Tamara Paulin all offered their expertise and comments along the way, as did Gloria Macarenko and Randene Neill.

Tammy Charles is my long-time associate and dear friend. She is always there to give five dollars worth of advice, even if I just ask for her two bits worth. You are priceless, TC.

Author and educator Bill Johnson wrote a most amazing book, *A Story is a Promise*. With his guidance and comments on the early manuscript, I was able to improve my writing, and understand the principles of keeping to the story, and tying up the loose ends.

Canadian humorist and author Gordon Kirkland has been most supportive. I particularly appreciate his interesting and off-beat way of seeing a situation, and for giving me tips and encouragement along the way. He's also the first Canadian board member of the Erma Bombeck Humor Writers Workshop, and he suggested that I join the humor writers group. Thanks for that.

Author Tim Bete, who is also the executive director of the Erma Bombeck Humor Writers Workshop, has provided just the right amount of encouragement and input on writing humor.

Author Susan Reinhardt, a true Southern Belle from Dixie, read the story and now thinks our families might be distantly related. That's all right with me!

Author Sylvia Taylor, Regional Director for the Federation of BC Writers, edited, asked questions and commented in just the right spots. I appreciate your support, and the good work on the manuscript's final edit.

Matthew Patton, Kelly Barrow, Kelli Shute and Eli Richart from AuthorHouse Publishing guided me along the road to publishing this book. Thanks for everything.

It is with the utmost of respect for the Aboriginal peoples in Canada that I wrote this story. The term of reference used for Tyee Mary and Old Joseph in *P.S. Don't Tell Your Mother* is in keeping with the timeframe of the late 1950's and early 1960's, when things were different than they are today. Or were they?

The Yellowpoint Lodge on Vancouver Island is where I finished the first draft of my manuscript. The second draft was completed at Clam Bay Farm on Pender Island, and the final edit took place on the island of Lesvos, Greece. No matter where in the world a person writes, it is important to write. I learned that in school. I would like to acknowledge three teachers from good old Skeena High for being the best teachers a kid from Terrace could have. Maybe they didn't even know it at the time. They are Hugh Powers, Ed Kenney Jr. and John Chen-Wing. From Hugh, I learned how to type. Fast. From Ed, I learned. He was clever in all matters of English, Social Studies and such. And from John, well, now. I learned that he really did like me after all, even though he gave me a detention every day.

Character List

Only 852 people live in Telkwa. Mom says that doesn't stop us from being friends or relatives with darn near everyone. And they're a bunch of characters.

Maggie Mulvaney, age 13, Terrace, B.C., Canada, the World

CHARACTER	RELATIONSHIP
Nana Noonan	Maggie Mulvaney's grandmother. Polly, Sue and Fran's Mom. Lives in Telkwa
Grandad Noonan	Maggie Mulvaney's grandfather. Husband to Nana. A very patient man
Maggie Mulvaney	Nana Noonan's 13-year-old granddaughter. Lives in Terrace
Fran Mulvaney	Nana Noonan's daughter. Maggie's Mom
A.E. Mulvaney	Maggie's Dad. Son of Grandma Mulvaney
Auntie Polly Hale	Nana's oldest daughter. Lives down the alley from Nana and Grandad, behind the John Deere tractor shop. Verna and Martin's Mom
Uncle Dan Hale	Auntie Polly's husband. Verna and Martin's Dad
Verna Hale	Nana's first granddaughter. Polly's daughter. A member of the Royal Canadian Air Force, she lives in London, Ontario, and marries Ben Winthrop at the wedding of the year in 1960
Martin Hale	Polly's 14-year-old son. Maggie's favourite boy cousin on the Mulvaney side, except for Willy Pike, but he's older
Auntie Sue Pike	Nana's middle daughter. Lives in Hazelton
Uncle Hank Pike	Sue's husband
Willy, Beth, Nan, Jane & Trudy Pike	Sue and Hank's kids, Age 25, 24, 22, 15, and 10
Chico & Spotty	Nana & Grandad's two dogs
Tippy	Maggie's only dog
Grandma Mulvaney	Maggie's grandmother. A.E.'s mother. Lives in Telkwa
Uncle Rob Mulvaney	A.E.'s oldest brother. Lives in Terrace with his family
Aunt Rene Mulvaney	A.E.'s sister-in-law. Rob's wife, Robbie and Annie-Lee's Mom
Robbie Mulvaney	Maggie's cousin, Rob & Rene's son, age 14
Annie-Lee Mulvaney	Maggie's cousin, Rob & Rene's daughter. Maggie's favorite cousin, age 12
Auntie Meryl Sandburne	A.E.'s only sister, who is smack-dab in the middle of the six Mulvaney boys. Owns the Telkwa Café with her husband
Uncle Martin Sandburne	Meryl's husband
Uncle Rick Mulvaney	A.E.'s third youngest brother. A prospector, he splits time between the mountains and Terrace

CHARACTER	RELATIONSHIP
Uncle David & Aunt Betty Mulvaney and their kids Joan, Wynn, Davie and Jamey	A.E.'s brother, born between A.E. and his sister Meryl. He and his family live in the sunny south. He owns a plumbing business and Betty does the books. They visit the north every so often, usually around Telkwa Barbecue time
Uncle Geordie Mulvaney	A.E.'s second youngest brother. Lives on the Queen Charlotte Islands. He's a heavy duty mechanic, and inherited Grandma Mulvaney's baking skills
Uncle Harry & Auntie Pearl Mulvaney	A.E.'s youngest brother. He's an electrician, and lives in Prince Rupert with his new wife and baby son
The Jehovah	He visits Nana Noonan every week, rain, shine, snow or sleet. A Jehovah's Witness
Constable Reems	Fresh-out-of-Regina Royal Canadian Mounted Police officer. Responsible for the Telkwa and Round Lake District. Stationed in Smithers. Gets to know and like Nana pretty well
Trapper Art Lawrence	Uncle Rick's best friend. He's a real outdoorsman, a prospector and animal lover. He earned his nickname the only time he and Uncle Rick went hunting with Nana. Somehow Art got his foot and his gun caught in a trap
Tyee Mary	Native Indian woman. Nana's best friend. Lives on a Reserve near Round Lake, just outside of Telkwa
Old Joseph	Tyee Mary's husband
Simon, Peter, Andrew, James, John, Philip, Bartholomew, Thomas, Thaddaeus James, Matthew J.	Tyee Mary and Old Joseph's ten sons, named after the twelve apostles. They are all good friends with Nana, Grandad, and the Mulvaneys. The boys are scattered all over the Pacific Northwest
Little Mary, Josephine & Eve	Mary and Joseph's three daughters. They live on the Reserve near their parents
Martha & Hilda Throckmorton	Twin sisters. Both hairdressers. Martha owns Martha's Heavenly Hair Salon in Telkwa, and Hilda owns Hilda's Hair Haven in Terrace
Ronnie Southam	Maggie's best friend since the day the Mulvaney's moved to Terrace, age 13
Mr. & Mrs. Southam & Wendy	Ronnie's parents and her older sister. Ronnie's Dad owns one of Terrace's Cadillac cars
Rusty Franklin	Ronnie's cousin on her Mom's side. A career Air Force man, when he gets older, age 17
Patty Phelps	Telkwa's Postmistress. Owns the Phelps part of Phelps & Saunders General Store in Telkwa. Grandma Mulvaney's bridge partner
Mrs. Ana Saunders	The Saunders in Phelps & Saunders General Store
Peter Phelps & Joel Saunders	Long-suffering husbands of Patty and Ana. They own the Telkwa Hotel and are very silent partners in the Phelps & Saunders General Store
Doc MacPherson	Telkwa's doctor
Mrs. King	Nana's bridge partner
Mr. King	Husband of Mrs. King. His expert cooking skills are what makes the beef so popular at the Telkwa Barbecue

CHARACTER	RELATIONSHIP
Uncle Jim & Auntie Yvonne & cousin Lou	Nana's brother and his family. Both Jim and Lou are loggers and they live in Terrace. Lou owns one of Terrace's Cadillac cars
Jack & Jessie Rose	Long-time family friends. Former owners of the Telkwa Café
Caroline Rose	The Roses' daughter, age 12; best friends with Annie-Lee Mulvaney
Janey Rose	Caroline's younger sister, age 6
Ben & Wee Mary Rollings	Long-time Telkwa residents and family friends with the Noonans and Mulvaneys. Wee Mary is Telkwa's shortest citizen. She can crack a softball from here to eternity. Played for years on the Telkwa Ramblers Team with Fran
Alice & Bobby Tarrant and their kids: The first triplets—Tammy, Dougie & Stephie, the regular kids—Alex, Charley, Sam, Rachael, Lorne, Tommy, Jackie, Arnie & Natia. The first twins—David & Janis, the second twins—Ricky & Michelle; the second triplets—Kathi, Bette & Debbie & the third triplets—Tim, Sara & Maxwell	Long-time Telkwa residents. Their house is big enough to hold a hundred on account of all their kids. Mrs. Tarrant said she wanted a lot of kids, and Mr. Tarrant was all for that. The kids range in age from 25-years-old, down to four months old. Many of the town's parties are held at the Tarrants. They host the Telkwa Toe Tappers Square Dance Club every Tuesday, of which most of Maggie's relatives and friends belong. The Tarrants oldest triplet just gave birth to the family's first grandchild—Shelley-Anne. She's ten-months-old. Her little feet have yet to touch the ground! Her Uncle Maxwell is just a year older than Shelley-Anne, and he is the most strong-willed little soul you'll ever meet. Good thing he is the last of the kids, so his brothers and sisters can keep him in check. Or try to
The Redferns and their twin daughters, Dale and Gayle	Farmers who live a few miles along Highway 16 East, towards Round Lake. They hold the annual Telkwa Toe Tapper Square Dance Club summer picnic and dance in their corral and barn. Gayle calls the Square Dances and is getting a reputation as the clearest caller in the Bulkley Valley. Even Mrs. Grammercy can hear her. Dale is Maggie's school chum from Telkwa. Active member of the 4H Farm Club
Jack Danford	Nana's solicitor. He and his wife Bernie and their four kids live in Terrace
Mrs. Hopkins	Nana's long-time friend and neighbor on the well side of her property
Vern Hopkins	Mrs. Hopkins' son. Helps Nana and Grandad with chores
Daisy Pahat	Mrs. Hopkins' daughter. Daisy, Fran, Rene, Polly and Sue all grew up together. Lives in Telkwa
Bill Buller	Long-time boyfriend of Daisy Pahat. His band, the Bulkley Valley Ranchers, is the most popular dance band in the region. They played at cousin Verna's wedding
Fern Pahat	Daisy's sister. Owns Terrace's fanciest dress and accessories store, Fern's Specialty Shop
Mrs. Strange	Nana's next door neighbor on the barn and outhouse side
Patsy Thomas and her husband Steve Scott	Grew up in Telkwa. Trained as a medical office assistant. Now the Manager at Northern Drugs in Terrace. Used to baby-sit for Fran and A.E. Both she and Steve love Maggie to bits

CHARACTER	RELATIONSHIP
Johnny & Marg Williams	Family friend from the early days. Johnny moved to the sunny south when he was a teenager. He seldom misses coming back to town for the Telkwa Barbecue. Marg is from back east. Together they own a horse and tackle shop. Johnny writes cowboy poetry
Mr. Thenhorne	Oldest man in Telkwa until he passed away
Mrs. Grammercy	Oldest lady in Telkwa. Nearly stone deaf on one side, and very hard of hearing on the other
The Stoddards; son John, daughters Janey and Wanda	Friends of the Noonan and Mulvaney families. Best friends of Patty and Peter Phelps
The Rannerfans; son Jimmy	Richest people in Smithers. They own the skating rink, the feed store and Super Value, and have a high opinion of their worth. Much higher than the residents of Smithers, Telkwa and the rest of the Bulkley Valley combined. Jimmy is a lighting expert. He does the lighting for the Smithers Skating Club annual Ice Follies on New Year's Day
The Dovers; daughter Eileen	Best friends with the Rannerfans. They are most likely the only people in the entire Bulkley Valley who have a high opinion of the Rannerfans. Mr. Dover manages the skating rink. Eileen Dover is the best figure skater in the Pacific Northwest
Those Stranges	The rowdy relatives of Nana's neighbor, Mrs. Strange. They live in a shack at the back of Mrs. Strange's property, real close to Nana's outhouse
Julie Bristle & Wilma Carp	Play for the Telkwa Ramblers Softball Club. Julie likes to sing; they both like to drink, and are always ready for a fight. No matter who with
The Dillards: Sons Ricky, Don, Tony & Perry, twins Adam & Jamie, daughters Pauline and Cara	Mrs. Dillard owns Terrace's only boarding house. Part of their family was lost due to Mother Nature and a slide on the road between Terrace and Prince Rupert
The Telkwa Ramblers	Women's softball team. Telkwa is big on ball. The women have won more division championships than any other team in the Pacific Northwest. Maggie's Mom Fran holds the record for most home runs. Ever
Round Lake Regatta	Held every July 1st. The sign on the turn off at Highway 16 and Round Lake Road reads: Round Lake Regatta every July 1st. 10 a.m. to 5 a.m. Boat Races, Kid's Races, Salmon Barbecue. Dance at Round Lake Hall, from 8 p.m. till who knows when, featuring Bill Buller's Bulkley Valley Ranchers. Free beer till the keg runs out!
Telkwa Barbecue	Since 1912, the Telkwa Barbecue takes over the Labor Day weekend. Highlights are a softball tournament, horseshoe tourney and the most famous beef on a bun in the whole Pacific Northwest, and maybe even the province of British Columbia. No one has ever argued with the townsfolk on that point. Once in a while, they throw in a rodeo for fun.
Smithers Fall Fair & Rodeo	Come mid-September, folks head down the road to Smithers with all their livestock, home preserves and horticulture and home economics entries. Maggie's family has entered and won many a prize at the Smithers Fall Fair

P.S. Don't Tell Your Mother

Look Me in the Eye and Say That

An Irish temper and accuracy with a gun is what got my Nana Noonan into trouble. She's taught me a lot. Although I've never shot anyone, I credit my sharp reflexes to keeping an eye on Nana.

I've learned it pays off to have a sense of humor, as Nana uses hers to get out of more than a few jams along the way. By setting bad examples around the town of Telkwa, population 852, Nana taught me it is important to be fair to your fellow humans. As long as they don't drive you to do something foolish.

I'm Maggie Mulvaney. I live with my Mom Fran, Dad A. E., and dog Tippy in Terrace, which is 150 miles away from Nana.

Three years ago for my tenth birthday, Nana gave me a box with writing paper and envelopes in it. And she gave me a fountain pen. Not the kind like in school, where you have to dip it in ink. A real one that holds ink inside it. And for my 12th birthday, I got some turquoise ink! I love writing Nana, because I like to do handwriting, and what she tells me in her letters is best kept on paper.

She doesn't much care for the telephone anyway. Nana says Telkwa is one big party line and the number of people who only hear half the story when they pick up the line is the way rumors start.

It's easy to write her and keep up on what's happening in Telkwa, because the mail only takes a day to go by train from here to there.

In the hundreds of letters she sends me, THAT DAMN JEHOVAH! is her favorite phrase.

She doesn't trust anyone who won't look you in the eye. Like that Jehovah. He is hell-bent on saving Nana. His high hopes on salvation

1

equal her intent to remain as she is: hell-bent on being herself. After all, she is an Anglican.

I like it that she's Irish. But she has a temper. There are lots of things that get her going. The Jehovah tops her list.

The townsfolk place bets on Nana and the Jehovah and when they will have their next 'set to'. Cash exchanges hands on a fairly regular basis.

Nana keeps me up to date on the real situation. There is more to it than the Jehovah and Nana not seeing eye-to-eye.

I understand more than I let on. Both Nana and I know that I can keep a secret and I'd make a good witness if I had to.

However, over this past year—almost too late—I have found out that when you give good advice, you can't always depend on it being taken.

I still have a lot to learn about human nature. Nana's a good start.

She is just half an inch short of six feet. Maybe the Jehovah got scared when he looked up at her. Nana isn't fancy. She wears a housedress, apron and sweater, nylons and no-nonsense shoes, and Martha, of Martha's Heavenly Hair Salon, does her hair every week. Nana always wears a bit of rouge on her cheeks and wears Bonne Belle Peachy-Crème pink lipstick. She smells of Noxzema, which makes her skin the softest of anyone in our family. Normal ends there. She is not like regular grandmothers.

She stands so straight and looks right at you with her sky-blue eyes. When she talks to you, she expects that you will listen and then have a good chat. I pity that Jehovah. He doesn't understand that Nana is very sweet. In her own way. At least she's nice to me and the rest of our family. She does have a way of raising one eyebrow so slightly that if you aren't really watching you know something happened, but can't put your finger on it. Dad says it's Nana's presence that scares the crap out of the best of men. Grandad won the prize for best man, then. He won't put up with much crap from Nana. That's why she spreads it around town instead.

She'll help anyone who is at their worst. She pitches in at all the town events, and does whatever she can for the Women's Institute and the poor. She goes out of her way to do something for anyone who is out of work, sick or sad. They'll tell you that it is Nana Noonan who quietly did the most for them.

Nana always tells us kids to lead by example and don't brag about it.

That's why I can't figure out why she doesn't like the Jehovah. The only thing I can figure is that because the Jehovah doesn't help anybody around town, and just tries to sell his religion to people—for free—Nana might think he isn't setting a good example. There's something about him that gets her going, and every once in a while, I will throw a prayer in at night for the poor Jehovah, just to put in my two bits worth and try to help even out the score.

It's not working so far.

Saturday, June 20, 1959
Dear Maggie:

That damn Jehovah was back here hammering on the door. I told him to get the Hell off my property, but he never has listened. He keeps leaving his "literature." He also has the nerve to suggest I need think about the future. It's his presence I'm thinking about. I toss his magazine over the fence. Once he makes it to the alley, he just tosses it back in the yard and takes off.

Grandad says that if it bothers me so much I should put up a sign on the fence. I won't. It's my property. He can come to the door, but he had better be a good runner because he's going to be on the hard end of my work shoes next time. He scares me a bit. Don't tell your Mother. Next thing she'll be up here sitting on the doorstep, ready to tell him off. I can tell him off, I just can't get him to bugger off.

Went over to Phelps & Saunders store today. Tyee Mary and Old Joseph came in on their buckboards. I guess old Tyee Mary wasn't feeling too good. She had to go to the toilet and asked Mrs. Saunders whether they had an outhouse. Yep, just out back, she says. Old Mary was off like a shot.

Then Patty Phelps, good Anglican that she is, came stomping in. She was all in a huff because Tyee Mary was doing her business by the back door. I guess Mrs. Saunders forgot to say that the outhouse is along the path, and to the right. Patty was in quite a state and the old gals ended up telling Tyee Mary off when she came back in the store. I told those busybodies to stop it, because Mary can't hear, so that could have been the problem. The fact that Mrs. Saunders is English, and mumbles, was more likely the problem.

Got a good deal on tomato soup. Had some fresh bread, some cheese and onion sandwiches and we had them with the soup for supper.

We've had a lot of rain here the last bit. Poor bloomin' raspberries don't know what to do. Those Stranges next door keep picking the raspberries and saskatoons and I'm about ready to call Constable Reems. The Stranges say if I put my 410 shotgun out of sight, they'd feel better. I say, if they stay the hell off my property, and pick their own berries, I'd feel better and we'd be even. Those beggars can only pick their noses.

Auntie Polly was over for tea this last Tuesday. We had digestive biscuits. I told her about the Stranges and she thinks I ought to fire a shot. She is still mad at Alex Strange for looking in her window and laughing when she was getting undressed in 1934. I guess she wasn't the best one to ask advice from. Uncle Dan says Polly knows from experience as they have those crazy yahoos next door to them. They stay up all night drinking and fighting. Guess I'm better off. At least the Stranges are too poor to buy liquor.

They're too stupid to fight, now that I think of it.

Love Nana

P.S. Martha died her hair a real sickly orange. No one knows for sure what happened. I think she left it on too long. Tell your Mother about Martha, but not about the Jehovah.

Orange Aid

Monday, July 6, 1959
Dear Maggie:

It was sure nice to see you and your Mom and Dad at the Round Lake Regatta last weekend. Don't worry. Not too many people saw you throwing up. I guess we should have told you that the barbecue salmon is rich. Your Mom didn't know you ate Cheezies and orange pop, too. All that orange stuff coming from such a tiny girl. You looked a bit like you'd been nibbling on Martha's hair. She has it a brown-y orange now, and it looks better. But not much.

Love Nana

Friday, July 10, 1959
Dear Nana:

Thank you for helping me last weekend. I didn't think I would stop puking! Good thing that most of the crowd was watching the boat race and you got me to the end of the dock.

We're pretty good here. I am going to a show tonight with Ronnie. It's called Ben Her and stars Charlton Heston and Jack Hawkins. There is supposed to be a lot of fighting and chariot racing and some lions trying to eat people. AND the men are wearing little skirts.

It's been pretty rainy. We want to go to Lakelse Lake. Mom says not yet because we'll get colds. It's already July!

Lots of Love, Maggie

P.S. Thanks again for kicking the dirt around me and making it seem like everybody throws up at the Round Lake Regatta. I love you.

What I didn't tell Nana, Mom or Dad is that I'd also had two Cokes because the salmon was salty and made me thirsty.

I've seen just one other person throw up before. It was one of Tyee Mary's sons. John had just made it out of the Telkwa Hotel Bar. I was on my way to the Post Office for Nana, and heard something fall against the wall. It was John. He didn't see me and I haven't bothered telling him or anyone.

A lot of the Indian people who go to the Telkwa Hotel Bar spend all their money on booze, and forget their families. I know lots of Indian kids who spend Saturdays in the park by the river, waiting for their parents to come out of the bar. Tyee Mary's family doesn't go to the bar too much, only to celebrate things. Nana says that Indian people can't hold their liquor. I disagree. John looked like he'd been holding a whole case of beer. Anyway, more white people spend their time and money at the Telkwa Bar than all the Indians in the region. They shouldn't be so fast to pick on the Indians.

If I looked like John did when I was at the Round Lake Regatta, I am glad that there weren't too many people watching me. I overheard Nana—when she was telling Mom about me at the Regatta—that she didn't think anyone could throw up for so long. I almost interrupted and told them about John, then thought better of it. John and his family have enough people going on about them drinking without me helping. It's not so much the getting sick, it's where you are when it happens. Both John and I were lucky. I had Nana and he had me to keep our big traps shut. Except when we were puking!

Friday, July 17, 1959
Dear Maggie:

I got your letter today. Don't worry. I threw up at the Round Lake Regatta once too, but it was from something else. I will tell you about it when you are older.

The garden looks real nice, and the dahlias and glads are coming up good. Hope you can come to visit for a bit. I saw your Grandma Mulvaney the other day and she has the other cousins here for the summer, even Joan, Wynn, Davey and Jamey from Vancouver. Your Uncle David and Auntie Betty Mulvaney will fetch them when they come up for the Telkwa Barbecue. Grandma says she can't have all of you, but looks to me like she has over half of them. Why don't you come up here and stay with us? You could see your cousins.

Lots of Love Nana

P.S. Tell your Mother

Friday, July 24, 1959
Dear Maggie:

When you come up next week, would you bring me two jars Noxzema and six cans of Pacific evaporated milk? They don't have any at Phelps & Saunders. Only that Carnation stuff and it tastes funny if you ask me. And 2 fine-tooth combs, some hairnets – your Mom knows what kind I like – and some Malted Milk bars, so we can have a treat when you get here.

See you soon.

Love Nana

P.S. Here's some money. The $20 is for you to buy something new to wear at school, and the $10 is for the things I need. Martin got $20, so did the Pike girls.

The Owl and the Bunny

Thursday, September 3, 1959
Dear Nana:

Thanks a lot for the nice time at your place. It was fun, and we hope that big old owl has stopped bothering the rabbits. Make sure you bring Bunny in the house at night, because she is my favorite. Mom says naming the rabbit Margaret and then calling it Bunny as a nickname has offended Margaret "Bunny" Jones. Oh, for gosh sakes, I say! We didn't even think of Bunny Jones when we named it Margaret. It was after Princess Margaret because she is so pretty and has black hair and so does Bunny.

I left my comb, brush, shampoo and two barrettes out by the washtub. Did you find them? Please keep them for me when we come up again. Mom had to buy me another brush and comb because my hair was so tangled when we got home. The gum Martin stuck in it wouldn't come out, even using an ice cube, so Mom cut a big chunk out of the back of my hair. For the first day of school, we pulled it back on the top part and it didn't look too bad. I have an appointment with Martha when we come up to the Fall Fair next weekend, and unless she dyes it, my hair will sure look better than it does now.

Love, Maggie

It must be hard to be an owl. Nana's bunnies are lucky. They sleep in a cage at night, and Grandad pulls a brown tarp over the mesh at the front. If you are still awake around midnight, and the moon is out, it is a good thing for the bunnies that they can't see what I've seen.

The owl always comes from behind St. Stephen's Anglican Church. He sure can fly. I'm not an expert on owls, but he is big. He looks like one of the floatplanes from Trans Provincial Airlines, coming in for a landing at Tyee Lake. First to the right. Then to the left. Just like the plane, it almost stops flying for a second. Swoop! Whoosh! He's past Nana's house and the bunnies are thumping like mad, and then screeching. I don't like it one bit. Always gives me goose bumps. I'm not sure who I feel sorrier for, the owl or the bunnies.

Nana keeps threatening to shoot the damn thing. She teaches all the kids in town gun safety, and is such a good shot that she could probably zing a bullet past the owl's ear and just scare it off. I talked to my cousin Martin about whether Nana would shoot the poor owl. He says that with all the yapping Nana does to us kids about safety and guns, and how we should only shoot if we are in need of food or it is grouse season, it is not very likely that she would lose her head and kill the poor owl. He is just hungry, and the bunny shack is like the Telkwa Café is to us. Why go to all the extra work to look for your food when it's being served up in a bunny shack café?

We've decided that Nana is a lot of talk. A whole lot, says Martin. I think she will do whatever she can to protect her property. Martin and I aren't usually up for betting on things like the rest of Telkwa is, but we both put up our allowance, just in case. Martin says no. I say yes, she's going to do something to that poor owl. I wish I lived closer and knew where the owl was so I could give him fair warning. This is one bet I am hoping I don't win.

Friday, September 4, 1959
Dear Maggie:

You'll be happy to know that the owl is not going to bother the rabbits at our place anymore. I was sick and tired of that damn owl scaring them so I stayed up late last night with my good friend, the 25.20 deer rifle.

Grandad went to bed around 10:30, after listening to the CBC national news. I went into your Auntie Polly's old bedroom overlooking the garden and the rabbit hutch. I opened the window wide and got a clear view of everything because the moon was out. At about midnight, the rabbits began thumping and making noise. Sure enough, a second or two later I heard the swish of the owl. He swooped in and down toward the hutch. That deer rifle is my favorite. I winged the owl right where I wanted to, and then spent most of the night fixing his wing. Grandad helped.

It is staying with us until its wing heals, and I won't take any crap from it. We have held its wings out, and the span is nearly six feet. A big bugger! Once it gets better, we're going to give it a free ride to Malkow Lookout and introduce him to some new rabbits, not ours.

Love Nana

P.S. Tell your mother that her mother is still a crack shot. Grouse season starts pretty soon, so she can come up and I'll give her a couple lessons before we head out. You can come too.

Little Dog Lost

Fall is my favorite time of the year. We've got lots of alder and poplar trees around here. The leaves turn bright yellow and the smell of them rotting on the ground is quite sweet, with a touch of dirt thrown in to remind you what is going on in our world. The temperature during the day can get up to 65° or 70° F. The air goes up your nose better in the fall. Each tree and piece of grass has laid off the heavy summer perfume, and stopped trying to impress the bees. In the summer, the leaves vibrate when the wind blows. It sounds like someone shaking a box of Kellogg's Corn Flakes. In the fall, they quiet down. That is because they are using all their strength, hanging on to the branches for dear life.

We love being in the outdoors in the fall. Nana takes us kids grouse hunting. We go south of town in the hills behind the coal mine. Nana says that the best grouse are at the spot where the poplar and alder trees greet their cousins the evergreens, which live at the foot of the rugged Telkwa Pass. We always get the best grouse there, so she's right.

Nana's two dogs tag along with us wherever we go. Chico is a black and white terrier and Spotty is a brown cocker spaniel-terrier cross, and she has the cutest freckles. Chico has an attitude. He is Nana's favorite, and their personalities are perfectly matched. Neither one gives an inch.

Sunday, September 6, 1959
Dear Maggie:

I am sorry to tell you that we have lost Chico and Spotty. They were with me when I was out hunting up the mine road with Martin and Tyee Mary. Something took their attention. They didn't come back for supper

10

like they usually do when they run away on the scent of something. It's been about three days. Grandad and I went out to the same area, and kept calling. All we could hear were the birds and now that fall is here, the nights are cold.

We sure do miss those pups.

Love Nana

P.S. Tell your Mother

Wednesday, September 16, 1959
Dear Maggie:

Thanks for phoning to check on Chico and Spotty. I was surprised when Chico made it home. He looks happy. Sure is sticking close. Makes us miss Spotty even more.

Love Nana

P.S. Thanks a lot for all of you coming up to help in the search for the dogs. I told Chico that you had helped look for him.

Thursday, October 1, 1959 (The day before my 63rd birthday!)
Dear Maggie:

Auntie Polly and I are sending you this sweater. It was supposed to fit Verna but since she's in the Air Force and wearing uniforms all the time, I decided to give it to you. Should go nice with your hair.

Martha has done it again. Got this bright orange stuff right on top of her head. Scares Hell out of Grandad. She should take a look in the mirror!

Still no Spotty.

Love Nana

Friday, October 2, 1959
Dear Maggie:

We wanted you to know about Spotty. She came home after 27 days! With a trap on her back leg. Skinny, too. The trap had gone right through her skin to the bone, but the bone wasn't broken. She must have eaten moss to stay alive.

Uncle Dan helped me take the trap off, and he drove us down to Dr. McPherson, who patched her up.

I got her a milk and bread dinner and she is still on that after a week. She is doing pretty well. Lying on the floor beside me right now. Chico was sure surprised. He kept walking past her and wagging that little stub of a tail of his. Grandad didn't say much, but I saw him bending over her this morning and talking to her.

Love Nana

P.S. Tell your Mother. Weather's turned. Sunny days and clear nights.

Monday, October 5, 1959
Dear Nana!

Thanks for the letter about Spotty! We are all happy to hear that she made it home. What was she doing out there all that time? Poor little puppy! I thought she had died and I was so sad and kept crying. Mom said to stay faithful or something but I thought she died. I'm going to give her a big hug when we come up for Thanksgiving.

What a good birthday present for you, Nana. I know how much you love your dogs, and even though Chico is so much like you, Spotty is cuddly and sweet like Grandad, and you love her a lot, too.

Say hi to Grandad, Uncle Dan, Auntie Polly and Martin. I love you lots and lots. Give Chico and Spotty a big hug from me and a woof from Tippy, too.

Love, Maggie

P.S. Oops. I am supposed to ask you what you want for your birthday and what we can bring from Super Value for Thanksgiving.

Oh. And I am supposed to say PHONE us collect when you get this. I don't know why. xoxoxo from Maggie

Roast Turkey and Cold Shoulder

We live over the Coast Mountain Range from Telkwa. The mountains around Terrace are high. The valley is narrower than the Bulkley Valley where Telkwa and Smithers are. My favorite mountain in Terrace is the Sleeping Beauty. It took me nearly a year to figure out which way her head is pointing, north or south. It was not until my Dad, A. E., drew the outline on the back of my social studies exercise book that I could make out which bumps were which.

The town has three levels: south of the tracks is the Keith Estate, then the main town area and the bench, where we live. I have never heard of the Keith family so I will have to ask someone how that name came to be.

Terrace is dusty. The Coast Range likes to pour rain on us. Good thing. We don't notice the dust as much. There are four paved roads. Two of them got that way because Queen Elizabeth and Prince Philip visited here for British Columbia's Centennial in 1958. We have two stoplights, both on the main drag, Lakelse Avenue. Both are a block away from each other. I never figured that out. Why not put a light on another street, and make it easier on drivers trying to get between the sporting goods store and the Super Value? Dad says it was to impress Queen Elizabeth and the Prince. We saw them come through town, and both lights were red. Their convertible just drove right on through, so now I have to talk to Dad about his theory, and ask around town about the stoplights.

Logging trucks come right through town, driven by the fathers of most of the kids I go to school with. These guys are tough. They comb their hair like Elvis or Buddy Holly and wear suspenders with their pants cut off just above their boot tops. They smoke Players or Export A. Some

13

of them smoke Sportsman, in the nice yellow packet with a fishing lure on one side, and a different fish on the other side. You can collect the packets, and win valuable prizes. Their wives work hard keeping them in lunches, and doubly hard to keep their kids noses and clothes clean. The guys like to go to the Royal Canadian Legion on Saturday with their wives for a bit of dinner, a lot of drinks and a few dances.

On Friday nights, the Lakelse Hotel Bar or Terrace Hotel Bar get busy, especially on payday. I heard Dad telling Uncle Rick that if he was thinking of going to the Lakelse Bar, he had better take his hard hat with him, or sit with his back to the wall and his bum half on the chair so he could dive under the table when the action gets too much for his personal safety.

Just a couple of weeks ago I heard my best friend Ronnie's Dad tell my Dad that two of the loggers' wives were hitting each other over the head with beer bottles. All five of Terrace's RCMP had to come to break it up. One of the RCMP got a bonk on his head, but he's used to it. After he learned his lesson and was hit, he just held on to both of their foreheads as they swung at each other.

The two ladies were stitched up at the hospital. Luckily, they made it back to the bar in time to have a nightcap, and watch their husbands get into an argument about which one of them got the most stitches. Next thing you know, the same RCMP is back—he called in another RCMP to break the guys up, because the wives had devilish looks on their faces, and fresh beer bottles in their hands.

Terrace is the "Hub of the Pacific Northwest." Telkwa is – Telkwa. It is fifteen times smaller than Terrace. Uncle Rick told me that, and he expected me to figure out how many people live here. Ronnie and I rode our bikes down to the outside edge of town to find out. All we did was have to turn around a bit and read "Welcome to Terrace – Hub of the Pacific Northwest – Pop. 15,000." I think they must mean the whole area, because from where I see, there are NOT 15,000 people in Terrace. Maybe the whole Pacific Northwest has 15,000 people, and that is what the sign means.

When we leave town to drive up to Telkwa, we take a good lunch with us, plus everything we will need in case of emergency. So far, so good. The only thing we've had to replace each trip is the roll of toilet paper that Mom packs in the glove compartment.

As the drive up is on partly paved road, we can make good time. When we hit the gravel patches, it is slow going. Not counting pee stops, the trip usually takes about three hours.

We eat our lunch along the way. Sometimes we stop in Hazelton at Aunt Sue and Uncle Hank Pike's place. They live a couple of hours from Terrace, so it makes a nice break and we can stretch our legs. We often have a cup of tea or coffee. Uncle Hank always has a few jokes to tell, and I love watching him laugh and wipe tears from his eyes when he gets near the punch line. Aunt Sue keeps busy, and my cousins Trudy, Jane, Nan and Beth are coming and going so the house is happy. Willy Pike is in the Canadian Air Force now. He lives in Ontario, and will be going overseas for peacekeeping soon.

When we travel to Telkwa, we always have fun. Grandma Mulvaney lives in Telkwa, too, so my cousin Annie-Lee Mulvaney usually rides up with us, while my dad's brother Rob, his wife Rene and my cousin Robbie go in their car. Annie-Lee and I sing songs, play games, or ask questions. Dad says his favorite game is for us to see how long we can be quiet. Every few minutes, I take it upon myself to ask him how long we've been quiet, just to keep Dad happy.

Highway 16 is the road that runs 2,175 miles from Winnipeg, Manitoba, to Prince Rupert and across the water to Massett on the Queen Charlotte Islands. We're at about mile 2,000 then, because Rupert is 90 miles from Terrace, and I'm giving the benefit of 85 miles between Rupert and Massett. I won't mention this to Uncle Rick, or he'd have me on my bike, riding all over trying to figure it out.

The only reason drivers and their passengers realize that there is a real town upon them at Telkwa is because there are three tight corners to make it around before the drivers continue west on the mostly straight stretches of road heading to Smithers, and beyond.

Anyone who has been through Telkwa knows that it is a cute little town. Anyone who has been through Telkwa also knows to get ready for the next corner, and stand on guard for farm equipment, stray dogs and Patty Phelps, the postmistress. She charges through town in her little Anglia Mini. Telkwa has only two stop signs and Patty has never been seen at those two corners.

Patty is the same size around as she is from head to toe: About four feet, eleven and a half inches. Her husband Peter had to put big blocks of wood on the Anglia's gas, clutch and break pedals, so that Patty could reach them.

I only rode once in the front seat of Patty's car. Since then, I happily sit low in the back seat, so as not to be thrown through the "wee window" of the Anglia. The roads may be mostly straight in Telkwa but it is amazing how Patty can make you feel like you're driving on a winding road. The sharp curves on the Telkwa patch of Highway 16 are easy for Patty, because she just goes to the far side of the corner and cranks the wheel the opposite way she is headed. Luckily, for her, the roads aren't that busy, and everyone who lives in town watches out for her. And themselves.

I think it would be a good idea to put up a big sign at the start of town: "Welcome to Telkwa, Pop. 852. Watch out for Patty Phelps in her Anglia and don't hit Nana Noonan's dog Chico. He likes to chase the Anglia."

Chico was waiting for Nana outside Phelps & Saunders store one October day. As any smart dog would do, Chico took advantage of the late fall sunshine. He was curled up near the log that stopped Patty's Anglia from hitting the front of the store. Too many customers complained that the canned goods got knocked off the lower shelves when Patty parked at the front of the store, so Mr. Phelps had one of the Telkwa loggers come by and deliver a two-foot wide, twelve-foot long fir tree. I named it Douglas. The whole town agrees it works like a charm. Mr. Phelps is happy because he doesn't have to pay his staff to restock the shelves every day or so.

Patty did her usual park job. Whap! Right into Douglas. Everyone in the store jumped and hollered when the Anglia let out the biggest backfire of its career as a car. Chico jumped the highest. He hates it when Patty's Anglia backfires. He ran around and around the car, barking his head off. Patty struggled out of the car, smiled at Chico, popped into the store, delivered the mail and then got back in the car in the same fashion: not that attractive, if I may say so. There's a lot of rear end to haul out of that little car and it's pretty hard to watch from my height.

Patty moved a bit faster than normal because of Chico's low growling and snapping at the left front bumper, which was right opposite where he had been laying. The only thing separating Chico and the car was Douglas Fir.

As Patty pulled away, Nana caught sight of Chico, leaping up over Douglas, right on the tail of the Anglia. Chico followed Patty, barking like a fool. She stopped at the end of town, and the Anglia shuddered and backfired again. Chico was hoarse from barking, but not too tired to lift his leg and pee on the tire closest to the exhaust pipe. He was still mad when he got home, and Nana says he growled and glared at things for a few hours.

Chico got over being mad at Patty when she brought him a nice jar of double cream when she delivered the Thanksgiving turkey to Nana.

We always eat Thanksgiving dinner at Nana and Grandad's, then we all cut across the alley to the Anglican Church yard, struggle with the big gate, and zip across Highway 16 and over to Grandma Mulvaney's, because she makes the best pumpkin pie in the Pacific Northwest. And everyone says that Grandma's lemon meringue pies are what legends are made of.

Wednesday, October 14, 1959
Dear Maggie:

It was sure nice to see you at Thanksgiving. What a treat to have dessert at Grandma Mulvaney's. Her pies get better every year. I think it is because of the shot of rum she adds to the pumpkin mixture. Though she never drinks, she sure can do wonders with booze and pies.

Tell your Dad that I hope his arse-end is better after he froze it on the bed upstairs. We should not have sent him up there without a hot water bottle. He's too skinny anyway. Grandad says you need some meat on your bones, too.

We went to Smithers with Dan and Polly. That damn Jehovah was on the corner by the Post Office. He should have stayed in the south and not come up here. We don't need any more of those types. He ought to go save himself, because he needs something to do. Grandad says to ignore him but it is darn hard when the Jehovah has his foot in my door and is telling me I need to read his magazine and see the world the way it really is. I was thinking about telling him off but Uncle Dan grabbed me by the arm and told me to move my arse towards the door of the Super Value or he'd be hopping in the car and leaving me there with nothing but the latest copy of the Jehovah's magazine to entertain myself. Before I could answer, we ran into Mrs. Dover and Mrs. Rannerfan and I decided to show them that I am the lady they think I am. I said, "Thank you Daniel, for helping me up on the steps of the Super Value." Then I added to the ladies that Dan is one of

*the best sons-in-law I have. They hardly had gotten around the corner when
I heard them laughing. Those damn busy bodies. They'd been watching us
from across the street.*

*We got some nice roast beef from the store anyway. Cooked it up with
peas and potatoes and made Yorkshire pudding. Polly and Dan had some
with us and took a bit home to Martin.*

Love Nana

P.S. Tell your Mother

Thursday, October 15, 1959
Dear Maggie:

*Thanks for the nice drawing of Chico and Spotty. Auntie Polly did up
some fresh tomatoes that were bruised from P & S Store. I had some with
toast. Grandad is going to mail this now, so I'll say good-bye.*

Love Nana

Shit-Disturbers Anonymous

Once we stuff ourselves on turkey for Thanksgiving, we like to spend most
of our time deciding what we'll do for Halloween. My best friend Ronnie
and I really dress up. We like to help make our own costumes. Our Moms
sew, and we add the decorations.

It is around Halloween that Nana begins her annual fretting. Dad says
she is Telkwa's unofficial shit-disturber.

Nana brings it on herself. With her Irish ways, she will curse and
bless something at the same time, tell a funny story or make a comment

that has everyone screeching with laughter. Then two seconds later, when they're wheezing and wiping tears from their eyes, she'll call them a stupid 'booger' and tell them just how dumb they are. Nana gets away with it, because she always tells the truth about the person. It isn't until she's moved on to the next poor 'booger' that the first one realizes he or she has been made fun of, because they usually agree with Nana and haven't had time to reply.

Each and every one of the townsfolk has been on the firing-end of Nana's tongue at one time or another. Since they have few chances for getting back at her, they naturally chose October 31 as the night to honor Nana Noonan.

The race is on to see who can knock over Nana's outdoor toilet and disturb her shit. She bitches about what might happen, and I think she gives everyone ideas.

Nana says that her family lets her down, and won't help her protect the family outhouse.

My Uncle Dan half-heartedly tries to guard the toilet, but he is a member of the Telkwa Volunteer Fire Department. Nana can't expect too much from him, especially since the Fire Department puts on the town's annual Halloween fireworks display. Auntie Polly stays home. It isn't her style to sit outside any night, let alone October 31.

Grandad faithfully guards St. Stephen's Anglican Church. He's spent every Halloween looking after the church since he moved to Telkwa in 1922. Besides, he says he's not going to freeze his arse off standing in the alley watching an outhouse.

Aunt Sue Pike is busy with her kids trick-or-treating, and she doesn't drive. Uncle Hank won't drive on Halloween. Neither one of them wants to freeze their arses off either, so Nana's out of luck from their end.

The interesting thing to me is that Nana and Grandad actually do freeze their arses off half the year, because they have never gotten an indoor toilet.

With the rest of the family busy every Halloween, that pretty well leaves my Mom to guard the townsfolk from Nana.

A lost cause from the start.

October 30, 1959
Dear Maggie:

I am starting this today because I know your Mom will only have a couple days here when she comes up for Halloween. I sure am thankful she can stay with me because I hate the shenanigans that go on. The whole town knows it. I think the Stranges must listen in on the phone when I talk about it to Auntie Polly. Grandad is going to be at the church, watching it, so I am glad your Mom can be here.

November 1. I am finishing this letter so your Mom can bring it back with her. You'll have heard about the outhouse by now. Bloody Strange kids! I'm sure it was them. We had to get the Telkwa Volunteer Fire Department to help right the poor toilet. Those fellows are a rude bunch. I told them to save their laughs for when they saw themselves naked in a mirror. The buggers. They just wouldn't give up! And Uncle Dan is the worst. He was laughing so hard he had tears streaming down his cheeks. He just said it was because of the smell. He knows I know better. Honestly! My own son-in-law!

Good thing we have the pots in the house. Grandad says it was easier to empty them with nothing but the hole in the ground.

I'm sending you this money so you can buy some clothes for winter.

Love Nana

P.S. The fireworks at the park were pretty. I'm sure that's when the Stranges knocked over the outhouse.

Wednesday, November 11, 1959
Dear Maggie:

We had a real good Remembrance Day service. Except that Jehovah walked by the service, too! He mumbled something about not meaning to be there because he doesn't believe in war, and that he hoped I could take time out of my busy day to read what he left me last Saturday morning. Damn him. We left early to get the church stove going and I put a few bits of greenery in a vase by the altar. That's when he must have slipped into our yard.

Grandad and I saw Dale Redfern's Mom, and she says hi to all of you. Dale's been busy with 4H Farm Club and a calf. They call it Stew. Going to be a big shock when Dale figures out why.

Getting real cold here. It has already snowed on Malkow Lookout.

Love Nana

P.S. Don't tell your Mother about the Jehovah.

The Solitary Saviour

Nana and the Jehovah's ongoing feud is the talk of the town.

I was staying with her the first day he paid a visit. He is a very stout, slightly bug-eyed, shorter fellow. He combs the hairs that still live on his head up from the bottom of his neck, dangerously close to his left ear and then back towards the right side. I don't know what he uses, but most times the hairs stay still, even in high winds.

The way he acts doesn't help him one bit, either. When he talks, he won't look at you. He blurts out what he has to say. He always has spit on his lip, but no one else seems to notice that but me. The spit kind of gathers in both corners of his mouth, and he gets this funny bubble of white stuff in the middle, which gets bigger the more he talks. Makes me have to look away. I try to be polite, because Nana and Mom and Dad taught me good manners. Something about him bugs me. It is all I can do not to turn tail and run the other way when Nana sends me to pick up the mail and I have to pass him on my way to the Post Office.

He works cleaning the Telkwa Hotel lobby after everyone has left for the night. Nana says that working nights doesn't do much for his social appeal. He stands on the street for most of the day, and no one else takes the time to talk to him. At least Nana talks to him.

Patty Phelps, who is his employer, landlord, and knows everybody's business because she is Telkwa's postmistress, says that he never buys stamps, uses the phone or gets mail, outside of a few copies of the Watchtower from The Jehovah's Witnesses.

Friday, November 13, 1959
Dear Maggie:

That Jehovah was back and I ended up phoning Constable Reems. The beggar kept holding the door and wouldn't let me shut it. Grandad was over at the church and I tried to pretend he was here. The Jehovah said he saw Grandad leave, and then he told me I was a liar and a sinner to boot. That did it. I went back inside the kitchen and showed him the shotgun. I didn't think eyes could bug out like that. He sure got up a head of steam then. I had the chance to shut the door and lock it. Before he could do anything more, I phoned Polly and she said I should call Constable Reems. So I did. He can't come over unless the Jehovah touches me or unless I want to go to Smithers and make a complaint. I'm going to think about it.

Love Nana

P.S. Don't tell your Mother! I'm telling you because you were here a couple times when he paid me a visit, and I need a witness. Keep this letter.

Tuesday, November 17, 1959
Dear Nana:

Thanks for the money. I sure hope you are OK. That Jehovah man is not very nice. I could send him a letter and ask him to stop bugging you, because you are already an Anglican. Do you have his address?

Love, Maggie

P.S. Maybe if you were a bit more polite to him, he'd be nicer to you. Don't worry. I have put your letter in the bottom drawer with my diary, which is LOCKED. And Mom already knows because she got a letter from Auntie Polly.

Friday, November 20, 1959
Dear Maggie:

 I told Polly to keep her nose out of my business. She's mad at me now, and I want your Mom to talk to her when you come up for Christmas. Grandad says that Polly and I have always been equally stubborn. Black is white, he says. The Jehovah is going to Vancouver for a few weeks on a course, so I can go about town with relief. We've got fourteen coming for dinner and maybe twenty if Sue, Hank and the girls come. Willy is back east and won't be able to get a pass. He likes the Air Force and leaves for Germany or Cyprus soon for peacekeeping. Wish he could come here in his uniform and help me out with the Jehovah.

 Weather is pretty good. We have a couple feet of snow and it's been clear. Lots of kids skating at the rink, so bring your skates. Tell your Dad to bring something soft to lie on. He's got to sleep in the same room as last time. We checked the beds and that bed is the softest. The beds can't help it if they are hard or half-frozen. I'll turn on the electric heater in your room before you go up to sleep. You get the cot by your Mom and Dad. Be sure to get here in time for the Carol Concert on Friday night.

Love Nana

P.S. Tell your Mother that I got a turkey and ham ordered, and she can get the vegetables with me when you get here because I want to go to the Super Value in Smithers for them.

Hot Time In the Old Town

We spend Christmas with both sides of my parent's family, usually at Nana and Grandad's. Uncles, aunts and cousins, and more than a few friends arrive around lunchtime. There is a bit of drinking, a lot of talking and laughter, and the cooks — my Mom and aunts — each get a bottle of red wine to polish off over the course of the day. We have a big turkey dinner. Bread and herb stuffing, mashed potatoes, gravy, peas and carrots, candied yams, Brussels sprouts, creamed corn, cranberry sauce, pickles and olives. Outside of the turkey and dressing, I like the pickle tray best. When I was little, I would park myself in front of the tray, only to realize that it moved around the table once everybody else sat down. When I was six, I caught on. I asked Santa for a can of black olives. He marched right down to Phelps & Saunders Store and picked up a can for me. I forgot to ask the year I was seven, and made up for it when I was eight. I asked for a tin of smoked oysters, saltine crackers and black olives. Santa was my best friend from then on. He granted my wish and I am a big believer to this day.

All the uncles take over the kid's new toys. When I was eight, I got a dart board and a hockey game. Except I never got a chance to play with either until January 3, when all the relatives went home and my Dad went back to work.

To stay at Nana and Grandad's is always an adventure. We kids are often put on guard duty for the Jehovah. Winter visits make it more like an Arctic expedition. We are posted by the door in the kitchen, perched on one of the two wooden stools, leaning at a left angle. The windows are always steamed up and the edges are frozen with ice. The grandchild's job is to keep a small hole defrosted, so that when she thinks about it, Nana can have a quick peek out into the porch and up the walkway towards the gate. Not once have I ever seen the Jehovah. I've been on duty since I can remember. It makes Nana feel better to know we're on her side, though.

Once the party and the laughs are over, those of us staying the night get serious before we head upstairs. The felt beds hold moisture and freeze up like Telkwa's two rivers. Nana never realized how hard the beds had become until she had a dizzy spell last fall and had to lie down on the bed that my parents use. After that, she's been slightly nicer to my poor Dad. He's a skinny guy, and he despises her bed almost as much as Nana despises her Jehovah.

Tuesday, December 15, 1959
Dear Nana:

I can hardly wait to see you, Grandad, and everybody. I hope you like this Christmas card, because Ronnie and I spent half the day on Saturday in Northern Drugs trying to pick the nicest cards. Patsy Thomas says hello. She helped us look for your present. She has been working at the drugstore for ten years now, and Mr. Manson, the owner, took her out for lunch to celebrate the day we were there. I miss Patsy babysitting me. This is the second year I haven't had to have anyone stay with me, and Patsy was my favorite. She's really nice and we always have a good laugh. If I was older or she was younger, we'd probably be best friends.

I'm bringing my skates and I hope to get a tobogon. Is that how you spell it? Tell Martin that I will go carolling with him and the other kids on Christmas Eve.

Love, Maggie

7 p.m. Saturday, January 2, 1960
Dear Maggie:

Thanks for helping so much when you were here. You're getting to be a good kitchen help, and I am glad you like to learn about cooking. That was funny when Uncle Rob spilled the turkey gravy on his new shirt and pants, eh? He probably did it on purpose, because he doesn't like to get dressed up. It took us a couple days to clean up after you. Boy, there was a lot of paper to burn.

Speaking of burning, and I'm not, but tell your Mother that the wallpaper around the chimney is only a few dollars to replace and the pipe is not too much either. It was lively here when the Telkwa Volunteer Fire Department arrived, wasn't it?

I knew that your Mom would go back to our house from the party at the Fire Hall to check on you kids just before midnight. When the call came into the hall, we were surprised that it was our place, because just then your Mom was telling me she'd been home a few minutes before and everything was fine. Your Mom sure can run! All those years playing ball paid off. She beat the fire truck and Uncle Dan prides himself in speedy driving!

I was very proud of you for making sure that all the kids had something warm on them when they went outside by the barn. Martin was very good, too. You all were.

We could see the fire out of the chimney from Polly and Dan's and that's a ways away! You kids did the right thing, and thanks for grabbing my purse and your Great Grandma's picture. It's the only one I have.

That was a good holiday and the house is quiet now.

Chico and Spotty are lying by Grandad's feet and he's listening to Hockey Night in Canada on the radio.

Love Nana

Sunday, January 3, 1960
Dear Nana and Grandad:

We made it home yesterday in 3 hours! I miss you already.

Thank you for the toboggan for Christmas. It was a lot of fun to get Martin, Beth, Nan, Jane and Trudy on with me. Dad says he can fix it because when we hit the rock, it split right down the middle and will either be two skinny toboggans or one repaired one when he's done with it. I hope Martin can walk better now. He wanted to be at the front.

Ronnie and I went to see Carry on Nurse and we had popcorn and a Coke each. We all laughed like heck. Mom and Dad drove us, and ended up staying for the show because everyone was talking about how funny it was. You would have laughed, too. I used the money you gave me. I also got two books to read.

We are going to Uncle Rob and Auntie Rene's for Sunday dinner tonight. He didn't laugh like we did when Dad told him we'd bring the gravy. Auntie Rene told him not to be so rude to his brother, but I couldn't hear what he said back at Dad.

Before dinner, Annie-Lee, Robbie and I are going to make a skating rink in the back yard at Uncle Rob and Auntie Rene's. The temperature is so cold right now, the rink should be frozen solid by the time we finish desert.

Trapper Art is back in town, so he's going to come along for supper, too. He's been out in the bush and decided to come in for supplies. He is staying with Uncle Rick. Remember the time he brought the baby raccoon to our house in Telkwa? I still hope he could find another one. I loved that sweet little raccoon. Except when it took a poo in the bookcase. Mom says it is not likely that Trapper Art will be bringing a raccoon to see us any time soon. He was none too happy when he had to clean up the raccoon and the bookcase. "Rocky" the raccoon now lives by Uncle Rick's here in Terrace. Whenever Trapper Art comes to stay, Rocky wanders by to say hello.

I like Trapper Art. He bought me a Toni perm kit for Christmas, because he says I have the prettiest hair he's ever seen. I don't have to use the kit, says Mom. Better to keep my hair the prettiest that Trapper Art has ever seen, because the last time I had a Toni, my hair and I came out looking as if we had spent a week in a really bad storm. Remember my school picture? Yuck!

Trapper Art seems to enjoy being with our family. He's a good story teller and I like that, too. Mom teased me and said she thinks I have a crush on him. He is kind of like the man I would think of marrying. He is strong, very nice, has a good sense of humor, and has blue eyes and blond hair. But he is already 23. Way too old for me, so Annie-Lee, Ronnie, and I are checking out a few of the older sisters around here, to try to keep him in town. I think he'd make a nice husband, anyway.

Love, Maggie

P.S. I might try the Toni, because it says 'soft curls' perm on the box.

Monday January 4, 1960
Dear Maggie:

I forgot to thank you for the nice gift. We're not sure where to put it yet, or what to do with it. I was wondering if you could send any instructions or the box it came in if you still have it. If you got it at Northern Drugs, I can write Patsy Thomas if you're not sure how it works. Grandad is stumped, and so am I.

Love Nana

P.S. Show this to your Mother.

Dear Fran: The cost for repairs was $3.98 for wallpaper, $10 for the new pipe and sleeve (and about $20 for the extra coal you stuffed in the stove to get it burning like that!). I was just kidding about the coal. Love from Mom

I am not sure what I gave Nana and Grandad, either. It is round and made from tin or aluminium. It has a little wooden handle on both sides and looks good and sturdy. It is about eight inches across and it came with a hook for hanging it up. It is supposed to do something easier. I think it is to make pancakes. Maybe. Or it is for the laundry. I'll be darned if I can remember what it does. I went back to Northern Drugs to see if I could find something like it in the bargain bin where I got it from in December. I've checked a couple of times, but I have never seen another thing like it. I'm stumped, too.

The Fur Follies

That was quite the Christmas and New Year. I was so scared when the chimney caught fire. The whooshing noise of the fire going up the chimney was so loud and the pipe was redder than Santa's hat. I think it was my Mom who helped the fire along. She didn't know that Nana had zipped home a few minutes before her, and had added about five big lumps of coal. Mom topped the supply off to a dozen and that's when the chimney caught on fire. She was mad at herself for not checking the fire and just throwing the coal in, because she didn't want to wreck her New Year's outfit.

Everyone was happy that Martin and I have had lots of fire drill training because our Dads are in the Telkwa Volunteer Fire Department. I'm just glad that it wasn't worse, because we wouldn't have been able to go to Smithers on New Year's Day. On second thought, we might just as well have stayed home.

For Christmas, Nana, Grandad, and Grandma Mulvaney gave us kids tickets to see the Smithers Skating Club and its Ice Follies Show. The kids who want to go on to win medals in skating put on quite the extravaganza! I read that on the program.

It's just that Nana put on a bit more of a show. Grandad decided he would stay home and it was a good thing he did. Though I'll bet that once he heard what happened, he kind of wished he were there.

We were all sitting in the first row because our family bought the most tickets.

I was between Nana and my cousin Martin, then all four of Aunt Sue Pike's girls. Next to Nana were Grandma Mulvaney, Annie-Lee, Robbie and Uncle Rick, who took us all in his Land Rover.

The show even had lighting, and the costumes were really beautiful. The little kids came out first. They didn't do much. Things were slow. Hard to get going when you're just learning, I guess. One kid came out and half walked, half skated. He was in front of us when he lost his balance and bent right over. All we could see was his rear end and two legs. He stayed like that for the whole song. Martin and I were screeching with laughter. So much that Patty Phelps, behind us, tapped Nana on the shoulder and told her to tell us to quiet down.

An older kid skated by and picked the little guy up. He was still bent over. What a lot of clapping went on for that kid. I hope he's too young to remember, or he will hate ice, skates and crowds forever.

The middle kids did little hops and were OK.

One girl fell from her highest leap and landed with a big face-first splat on the ice. She managed to get up and would have just had a wobbly finish, except that she headed for the wrong end of the rink. What a nice crowd. Everyone there hollered like Hell at her and pointed to the exit. Didn't help a lot, because we were all in the dark, and she couldn't see which way we were pointing. She eventually made it down the length of the rink, and as the lights were coming up, made a fast jump and landed inside the back stage area. The crowd was disappointed because someone pulled the curtain shut. I think she was badly hurt.

Then there was an intermission.

We should have left when the going was good.

The lights went out. Mrs. Rannerfan announced the winning number for the door prizes. No one could see their numbers and there was a lot of grumbling as everyone got out lighters or matches to check to see if they won a dinner at Beasley's Grill, or a set-and-curl at Martha's Heavenly Hair Salon, or the Grand Prize of $10 worth of hardware at Rannerfan's Hardware and Feed Store. We're still not sure who won.

The older kids came out all at once. The boys had on black pants, white shirts and black and red bow ties. All the girls were in red, with black bows, except one. Eileen Dover is blonde, and she had on a white ballerina skirt and sparkly top. She looked beautiful. Boy, can she skate!

She was zipping all over the ice, in and out of the other skaters.

The lights dimmed. All the skaters left the ice. Except Eileen. One spotlight operated by Jimmy Rannerfan followed her around the rink. The music was soft.

Eileen did a couple of jumps down the far end, and went backwards up the other side of the rink. She finished a nice jump at the top end, and then went by us on one leg, with the other leg so high up behind her it was like she was doing a standing-splits.

That's when the quietest part of the music came on.

Eileen glided past.

Nana let out a little gasp, and then said very loud, "Look at the fur!"

I didn't quite get what she meant until I glanced back at Eileen, in perfect splits by this time. I think I was the only one on our side of the rink not to catch on right away.

There were louder gasps, and then half the crowd took it upon itself to giggle, snort a couple times and laugh right out loud.

Nana couldn't leave well enough alone. She said, "Well...I only say what I see." The place went nuts. Martin fell from his seat and Nana was kicking at him. She hollered, "Get up, for Christ's sake, you're embarrassing me!" That did it for anyone else who wasn't already laughing. By then, the word had spread around the rink, and the whole place was hooting and clapping loudly.

The song was over. Eileen, knowing that she'd given her best performance ever, did an encore spin, a little jump, and the splits down the opposite side of the rink.

Nana, not to be outdone, bellowed, "See what I mean?"

Eileen got a standing ovation and while that was happening, Martin and I ran like Hell out to wait at the front of the rink. We made it behind Uncle Rick's Land Rover just in time to duck down and avoid the scene around Nana, who turned out to be the real star of the Smithers Ice Follies.

Friday, January 8, 1960
Dear Maggie:

There are some times in a person's life when a crowd gets them going. That happened to me and to Eileen Dover at the Smithers Skating Club Ice Follies.
At least I knew what I was doing.
I hope you're not too mad at me. When you think about it again, I am sure you will find it funny.

Love Nana

P.S. Tell your Mother that I wrote a note to the Dovers, so your Dad can still do business at their store when he comes back to Smithers. I also sent a card to Grandma Mulvaney. She doesn't have the same sense of humor as the rest of you Mulvaneys.

Kindling Spirits

Monday, January 25, 1960
Dear Maggie:

I haven't written lately because I have had a cold. Was chopping wood and didn't dress warmly enough. Just as I was coming back along the path from the woodshed, that Jehovah came marching along the alley. I told him he'd better not bother with the gate because I'd booby trapped it. He just laughed and came on in. I told him that I had weapons on me and he had better move his arse off our property. He didn't. I realize that I still have a good aim, even if I'm just chucking kindling. Got a few pieces on the go before Grandad came outside and hollered at me. Threw my aim right off. I hit the fence instead of that Damn Jehovah.

Grandad says that we act like a couple of school kids, going on like we do. Except that Jehovah should know better. I'm just protecting my property!

We had a nice roast dinner when Sue and Hank came up this past Sunday. They brought Hank's sister Mavis Pike with them. She's visiting from England. Tiny thing. Hardly eats. Must lose the weight with all her talking. Could hardly get a few hundred words in edgewise. We had a good visit anyway. Old Mr. Thenhorne died two days ago. Funeral is at the United Church. The Women's Institute is going to do the tea afterwards. I'm making some Nanaimo Bar squares and egg sandwiches. Polly is making ham and cheese sandwiches, too.

Love Nana

P.S. Tell your Mother about Mr. Thenhorne, but don't show her this letter (about the Jehovah.)

Wednesday, January 27, 1960
Dear Nana:

I am sorry to hear about old Mr. Thenhorne. His son, Thenhorne Junior, lives here in Terrace. He looks sad these days, probably because he is an orphan. His mother is dead, too. We sent him a card. I think I will ask for Nanaimo Bars at my funeral. That would be a very nice touch.

Love, Maggie

P.S. I'm not mad at you. I was just embarrassed. Half of Terrace has heard the fur story, and they keep asking me to tell it over again. Thanks a lot!

Wednesday, February 3, 1960
Dear Maggie:

It was rainy here this last week. Smells like spring, but when we went to church this morning, I nearly froze my privates. Guess that's how your Dad feels when he sleeps on the bed upstairs. Grandad and Mrs. Hopkins go over early to start the fire and get the place warmed up for Rev. Whiteside. He always looks like he came in from the sunny south. He has such rosy cheeks. Same color as mine after sitting on the pews for an hour. When we were leaving the church, the sun shone and the snow looked so pretty, glistening. There was a lot of melt on the ground by the time the sun went down.

We had some nice stew and a piece of cake for dinner. Polly was in a flap about their crazy neighbors. They can't get their times right. Sleep all day and party half the night. Fighting, too. Had a bunch of friends over on Saturday night. When the bottles launched into the air space around the yard, Polly went over to their front door – the one they never use – and she hammered on it. Some woman came to the door and she told Polly to Pi— off. Polly told her to go to Hell and to quiet down because her aunt up at the graveyard had called and asked if she could rest in peace. Uncle Dan heard the bellering and decided he had better break it up before things got mean. It took a bit, but Polly decided to come back home on her own as her feet were getting cold, on account that she was only wearing slippers.

A few of the neighbors heard everything and the church was pretty well informed by the time we got there.

Good thing Polly doesn't like to go to church, or it would have started up all over again.

Well, I had better get going. I hope you're doing fine in school. Martin likes math a lot, so if you are still having trouble with your long division, maybe he could give you some pointers.

Love Nana

Monday, February 15, 1960
Dear Nana:

Here is a picture of me at the United Church Valentine's Day tea. Uncle Rick got a new camera and he has been taking pictures of us kids. We think that my hair will be back to its wavy self by the time summer comes along. You should have seen it right after the Toni perm. I nearly cried. Thank gosh Trapper Art is back in the bush. I sure wouldn't want to see him when I look like this. If I pull my hair *out to its proper length, there is another 9 inches of hair. It was so tight on my head for the first week, I got a headache.*

Love, Maggie

Wednesday, February 17, 1960
Dear Maggie:

Thanks for the nice picture. Grandad and I have put it up on the bookshelf. Your hair looks very pretty, and you are right. It looks a lot shorter because of the perm. Martha could take a tip or two from you. She doesn't look as good as you do with a bad perm!

Here is a card and there is money in it so make sure you keep it safe and give it to your Mom and Dad on their Wedding Anniversary this Sunday.

Love Nana

Stew and the Telkwa Café

Mom and Dad owned the Telkwa Café in the 1940s before I was born. Once Dad joined the BC Forest Service in 1950, it went to our family friends, Jack and Jessie Rose. Then in the late 50s, Dad's sister Meryl and her husband Martin bought it.

The café is popular in town because it is an only, like me. The townsfolk take over the booths and stools, and enjoy real home cooking. My Mom and Grandma Mulvaney lead the tradition of Mulvaney family pies. We've operated a family bakery for over thirty years, and didn't know it. Grandma helped the Roses out off and on. Since Auntie Meryl took over, Grandma makes all the pies.

My favorite thing to do is sit up on the third stool from the end of the counter nearest the door, and swing around with my back to the counter. You get a great view of the entire café, as the pie mirror is even with that stool. If someone is on the stool when I get there, I glare at the person's neck, staring them down and hypnotizing them to move their arse off my property. It works, because nearly every time I get there, my stool is empty. Or the person gets up and moves to another stool.

Saturday, February 20, 1960
Dear Maggie:

We went to the Telkwa Café today, and ran into Mr. & Mrs. Redfern. They were telling us about Dale's calf, Stew. I guess one of the older brothers told Dale why the calf is named Stew, so Dale took off with the calf and had made it nearly to the top of the Mine Road Hill before someone spotted them. Dale was trying to make it to Patty and Peter Phelps's house, as Patty is dead against killing things. Anyway, there was hell to pay for Dale, and her Dad was some mad about having to take the calf home in the back of the truck. Dale rode with the calf, but couldn't stop it from kicking when it got worried about where it was going. Made a couple of nice dints in the side panel. Dale was in an awful state and Mr. Redfern wasn't having any more of her yowling. He took the calf to the barn and told Mrs. Redfern to take Dale into the house. I guess he was trying to decide what to do when the calf helped him make up his mind. It walked into the stall, lay down, and just looked at Mr. Redfern. He says that darn calf must have known it was going to get it, and was ready to go.

Mr. Redfern said a few words to the calf and went to get his gun. I guess the calf had second thoughts on its future, because all of a sudden it jumped up and ran around the stall like the Devil was chasing it. Mr. Redfern says he nearly jumped out of his skin and fell over backwards when the calf ran past him and out the barn door. The calf was nowhere in sight by the time Mr. Redfern picked himself up and made his way towards the road in front of the farm. He went to the house and told Dale to get in the truck as they were going to look for the G-D calf. He says that the look on Dale's face was so sweet he didn't have the heart to do much of a search, so they turned home after a quick tour of the town.

Patty Phelps now has a calf that looks so much like Stew it could BE Stew, says Dale. Sure makes us wonder how that calf made it all the way on its own up the Mine Road Hill, and to the Phelps farm.

Love Nana

P.S. Tell your Mother.

Sunday, February 21, 1960
Dear Maggie:

I hope your Mom and Dad are having a nice anniversary.

Forgot to tell you when we were at the Telkwa Café, your Grandma Mulvaney came in with four lemon meringue pies. She was helping your Auntie Meryl out as there has been a big run on pie and coffee because the coalmine has shut down for a week and everybody is going to the café for a B.S. session. The four pies went when we were there, and last we saw of Grandma Mulvaney was her heading back home to make two dozen more pies for tomorrow.

Uncle Martin and Auntie Meryl are sure working hard at the café. It's always busy and the food is good. They did a good job taking over from your Mom and Dad and the Roses.

Your Uncle Harry and Auntie Pearl Mulvaney were there, too. They were driving back to Prince Rupert after visiting Pearl's family in Vancouver. Their baby boy is cute. He has lots of curly blond hair, just like Harry had when he was a kid.

Love Nana

Spring Fevers

Spring is boring. The weather is crappy and cold. Half the time we don't get leaves on the trees until April. When the snow decides to buzz off, it takes its time. Ronnie and I spend many hours damming up the creek behind our house. I like school, but ended up getting sick for three whole weeks just after Valentine's Day. When I was allowed outside again, there were buds on the trees.

Monday, March 14, 1960
Dear Maggie:

We were glad to hear from you when you called last week. Sorry to hear about the chicken pox. Don't go outside without something on your head. You can catch a chill this time of the year, as it acts like spring and it is still winter.

Love Nana

Thursday, March 17, 1960 St. Patrick's Day
Dear Nana:

Happy St. Patrick's Day! Mom said I've been acting like a nasty little Leprechaun since I've been sick. Just in time for St. Paddy's Day, eh? My spots are red, not green, though.

Thanks for the nice card. I got it yesterday. I'm still off school because I am itchy. When I was sick, Uncle Rick gave me a puzzle. He and I did most of it over last weekend. He had chicken pox already, so it's OK for him to see me. I couldn't visit with Ronnie, because she hasn't had them until yesterday, so I guess I can go visit her when she feels better and is still just itchy. Mom says that is the problem with a small town. You don't even have to visit someone to catch something because it travels like gossip. Quick, and it hits you before you know what happened. Or something like that.

I had to get homework from school, and it is drawing a map of the world. I can't sit still too much because my whole legs and arms and stomach are still making me scratch.

I'm sending you and Grandad one of the three maps I tried to draw. I hope you like it. Africa isn't quite finished, and Australia and Antarctica aren't done too well, because just as I was doing the north of Africa, an itchy spell hit me. That is why you are getting the map. It looks a bit like Africa got Alaska and the Queen Charlotte Islands, doesn't it? The coloring is good, though.

I'm better now and there are NO germs on the paper because I left it outside for a few hours. It is really cold today, and no germ would live. I learned that in science just before I got sick.

Love, Maggie xoxo

My older cousin Verna is getting married to Ben Winthrop from London, Ontario. She's been in the Air Force since 1958. He's in the Air Force, too.

This is the first wedding of the grandkids. Nana, Auntie Polly, Aunt Sue and Mom have already made about ten long distance calls each.

Verna asked my cousin Jane Pike and me to be junior bridesmaids.

Mom says there is nothing like a wedding to bring out the beast in some folk. Nana had a good old-fashioned beastly moment just around the time she should have been choosing which dress to wear to Verna's wedding.

Saturday, March 26, 1960
Dear Maggie:

We got the news that Verna is to be married. I hear she's asked you and Jane to be bridesmaids, and Martin will be the usher along with Ben's brother, who is going to be best man. We all look forward to the day!

Tell your Mom that she has enough to do with making all you girls' dresses and Verna's, too. I'll go to Smithers and see what Mrs. Dover has at the dress shop. By getting married in May, Verna and Ben will have lots of nice flowers from the garden. Grandad has been talking to the lilacs.

We had a nice lunch with Grandma Mulvaney. She brought over a fresh loaf of bread, and we ate the whole thing. I'd made a stew the other day and we finished that off, too. Polly came by and brought some cake for dessert.

The weather is still chilly at night, but it's getting clearer each day, and a bit warmer.

Polly and I hosted the Women's Institute meeting here. We are planning to hold a tea at the library this Thanksgiving. We'll use recipes from the W.I. Centennial Cookbook. I hope you like your copy. The recipe for your favorite Nanaimo Bars is on page 171.

Had another visit from that Damn Jehovah. A few of the W.I. ladies were here after the meeting, as we were going over the recipes for the Thanksgiving Tea, and we got talking about what to serve at Verna's wedding dinner. By the time the meeting was over, my six cups of tea had caught up to me. When the ladies were getting their coats on, I headed to the outhouse. Just as I was turning the corner onto the outhouse path, the Jehovah appeared. Too bad, I didn't have a full pot with me. He'd stuck two magazines at the gate and was trying to make his way back down the alley before I saw him. I hollered and ran up to the gate and threw the magazines into the alley. Then I went back to do my business and the S.O.B. was waiting by the raspberry patch when I came back along the path. He said, "You must be saved, Mrs. Noonan." I did tell him that he doesn't have a clue about saving or he'd have gone inside the Royal Bank and made a deposit instead of standing outside it for all these years. I decided to go to Smithers next week and make a formal complaint to Constable Reems. After all, that Damn Jehovah was in MY yard. I never trespass onto someone's property.

Love Nana

P.S. Tell your Mother. She may want to make a trip up here and talk me out of going to the RCMP

Tuesday, March 29, 1960
Dear Nana:

Maybe the Jehovah is lonely. Patty Phelps told Mom that he doesn't even have a radio. He only seems happy on the days that he sees you. You might be the only person who talks to him! Of course, as you always say: "If you can't say something nice, don't say anything at all." Ha ha.

Love, Maggie

The Directions to Hell

Nana tells me more than I really want to know. Sometimes, though, she leaves an important thing or two out.

Our hairdressers are twins. We go to Hilda Throckmorton, of Hilda's Hair Haven in Terrace and Nana's hairdresser is Martha, of Martha's Heavenly Hair Salon in Telkwa. They know more about our family than we do. Hilda says that the talk in Telkwa is that Nana had a very loud chat with the Jehovah—just as her Women's Institute meeting was breaking up. She went to the outhouse as the ladies were putting on their coats and hats. The Jehovah was on his way in the gate as Nana came back along the path.

I can't think of a better show than Nana and the Jehovah, especially if she had an audience. And especially if the Jehovah was in her yard.

Hilda says that the Jehovah was trying to be polite, in his own way. Nana would have none of it. He blurted out, "Hello, Mrs. Noonan. What are you doing today?" She loudly told him that she and the ladies had just been taking an electricity lesson. The ladies looked as confused as the Jehovah until Nana said, "Yep. I figure that in about a month we'll have learned enough to string some lights to Hell, so you can find your way!"

Saturday, April 2, 1960
Dear Nana:

Boy, Mom was sure mad about that Jehovah. I guess she's up at your place now. Dad tried to tell her to stay home, but she said something about protecting the Jehovah, got in the car, and headed to your place.

I hope that your meeting went well and that Constable Reems was nice to you. I'd like to marry an RCMP when I grow up. We went to Madeline Redfern's wedding when she married that RCMP and it was very pretty.

Our dresses for Verna's wedding are pink. I am trying to grow my hair, but Mom says not to get my hopes up because hair grows only so fast, and the weeding is just two months away. Most of the perm from Trapper Art is gone, but it's still wavy, because my hair is wavy anyway.

Love, Maggie

P.S. Remember what you said to me about "DO UNTO OTHERS?" Maybe you could go to the Jehovah's room and deliver the Women's Institute Newsletter? We just got our Telkwa/Telwood W.I. issue and it's nice. We liked the write-up about Verna's wedding, complete with suggested recipes. Mom says to tell you that it is obvious who the editor was this month. YOU!

A Helping Hand

The whole town was shocked when a slide on the road between Terrace and Prince Rupert killed twelve people. I go to school with Ricky Dillard. His family isn't well off. Talk around Terrace is that they'll be really poor now. Five of their family was wiped out by the slide when it hit their only car.

Monday, April 4, 1960
Dear Maggie:

We heard on the radio that there was a big slide on the highway between Terrace and Rupert. The announcer said that some people died and it sounds like the Dillard family. I think they are the ones living near you. When you get this, have your Mom phone me so I can get their box number and I'll send them a card.

I always hate taking the train along that stretch where the slide happened. You be careful next time you drive that way to see Uncle Harry Mulvaney. I don't want anything to happen to you.

Love Nana

Saturday, April 9, 1960
Dear Nana:

We just got back from the big memorial service and luncheon for the Dillards. Their father, his brother, and three of the kids were killed, and so were seven other people. Dad went out to where the slide happened to help look for people. There was only one living thing left, which was a dog. Everyone from town has been helping Mrs. Dillard and the other kids. We told them that if there is anything we can do to help, we would. Mom says it isn't right now that they need us; it will be along the road. I think she meant in the next few years, too. I tried to talk to Ricky Dillard, but he says he doesn't want to see anybody right now. I hope something like the slide doesn't happen again. It is very sad and we all feel bad for the people left. Mrs. Dillard's box number is 1332. Mom says you might want to put some money in an envelope and not buy a card, just write a letter. Save money on buying the card and give it to Mrs. Dillard. They didn't have much money to begin with, and now they'll be a lot worse off with Mr. Dillard and the three older boys not being able to work because they are dead.

Mom says it is a good thing that spring is giving way and behaving like She should, as it might help cheer people up a bit.

The other people who died are from Rupert, and the Dillards had just stopped for a coffee, we think, because their thermos had hot coffee in it when they found the car. Uncle Harry knows the family who owned the rest stop because he pops in now and again when he's driving from Rupert to Terrace to see us. There were two construction workers there, and a young fellow from the Highways Department, too. It is so very sad for all the families. Mom and Dad are working with the Kinsmen on getting a trust fund set up for the Dillards.

Our class made a card and we all signed it. We took over some cookies for the luncheon.

We'll see you soon. I am glad you're coming here so I can show you my room. Mom just finished making my bedspread. It's lucky she finished it because she has to get busy on Verna's wedding dress. She says that I will have to wait until closer to the wedding for my dress. I hope she hurries up, because I want to try it on!

Can you bring Chico and Spotty with you? They could use a holiday, too. I hope we can go on the train somewhere. Maybe we could go to see the slide.

Dad says to tell you that there's a sale on mattresses at Terrace Furniture and you might want to have a look at them when you're here. I don't know why, because you already have beds!

Love, Maggie

Sleeping Beauty

Nana visits us often. She and my Dad see eye to eye, as long as my clever Dad keeps his distance. The sleeping arrangements at Nana's are a sore topic. Dad always makes sure that when she visits, Nana is sleeping on the softest bed in our house. It seemed fitting for my Dad to put Nana's beds out of their misery. When they were thrown out, they were in such sorry shape that the Telkwa Dump turned up its nose at the beds.

Terrace has more stores than Telkwa and Smithers combined. For clothes, we go to Fern's Specialty Shop. An ad in the Terrace Herald says, "The outfits and jewellery Fern brings in have a flair like no others in town." The Sears Catalogue outlet is doing a rip-snorting business this year, too.

Its Fern and her speciality shop that keep the female side of our family in the current styles.

It's a good thing that we Mulvaney ladies of Terrace keep our hair and nails done by Hilda's Hair Haven, because I think Uncle Rick likes Hilda. Northern Drugs and the Post Office are over a block away, yet Uncle Rick always parks his Land Rover in front of Hilda's Hair Haven. He usually pops in for a quick hello, and says he's checking to see if any of us Mulvaneys are in there. Hilda always has a Coke or a coffee for him. She's pretty, but she's kind of old, nearly 24. She does know how to do her hair just right. Not like her twin sister Martha.

Terrace Furniture is the place to buy stuff for your home. Whenever Nana visits, we make a point of going to the store to check out the latest in couches, chairs, tables and appliances. We never thought to try out the beds until this visit. It's hard work. Nana was so tired, she fell asleep! Dad got a good laugh when he borrowed an alarm clock from the houseware area.

He wound it up and put it real close to Nana's head. She came up off the bed, ready for a fight. Dad got one. He just doesn't learn, where Nana is concerned.

Monday, April 18, 1960
Dear Maggie:

I sure had a nice time visiting you and your Mom and Dad. The new mattress arrived today and Grandad was a bit ticked that I didn't bother to get one for his bed, just the one you folks sleep on when you come here. He doesn't need to know that your Dad paid for the mattress, OK?

Once I got on the train, I remembered my hatbox. It's on the bed in your spare room. Ask your Mom to put it on the train and we will pick it up at the station. My new dress made it home fine. The way Fern wrapped it in tissue, it hardly had any wrinkles when I took it out of the box.

Grandad must have missed me, because he had a bouquet of spring flowers for me on the table, and had really tidied the place up. And, he watered all my geraniums.

Love Nana

Chico and the Roast

Our dogs are very important family members. Once or twice, there's been a well-meaning and distant relative who thinks the dogs belong outside. One way or the other, if we find out, that relative pays for it.

When I was only four, my Uncle Rob Mulvaney and Nana's "wee brute" Chico got off to a bad start. From the day my Mom brought the ten-week-old pup home to Nana and Grandad, there wasn't much love lost between the dog and Uncle Rob. We were visiting Telkwa for a couple of weeks, so Chico went with Mom and me on outings. Shortly after his arrival, he was taken to the Telkwa Café to meet the regulars. Uncle Rob was over at the Café helping Auntie Meryl, my Dad and Uncle Martin chop wood. It was lunchtime. Meryl had made some soup and Grandma Mulvaney just delivered thirty loaves of bread. Uncle Rob did not think things through. He washed his face and hands, and looked for something with which to dry himself. I was in the kid's chair, and wee Chico was snuggled in a towel in a shoebox near the wood stove—and the washstand—safe and secure. The edge of Chico's makeshift bed was the first thing Uncle Rob touched.

With soap stinging his eyes and water dripping from his face, Uncle Rob flipped the towel toward himself with both hands.

It was a perfect way for Rob to cover his face with the warm towel. And a perfect way to catapult a one-pound puppy across the room. Wee puppies fly pretty well when they are tossed in the air.

That day, luck was with Chico. My Mom's reflexes from softball were in top form. Her left hand shot out, and she caught Chico with the grace of the North-Western Division Champ that she is. Mom would have put Chico back in the box, except Uncle Rob was using the pup's bedcovers at the time. She moved closer to Uncle Rob to explain the situation, and Chico added his two bits worth. He jumped from my Mom's left hand and for years and years, every time Uncle Rob saw the dog, he would tell the story to anyone who would listen: "Eye-to-eye with a one-pound terror." Chico was right pissed, and we still wonder how he managed to keep a firm grip on the towel, chomp quickly on Uncle Rob's hand, and wag his stubby tail at my Mom, who he worshiped from that day forward as his rescuer. In the split second it took for him to be plopped back in his rightful spot in the box by the fire, that little dog glared so hard at my uncle, I thought for sure Rob would fall through the floor or something.

Mom says that the look on Uncle Rob's face was the best. His eyes widened. One eyebrow went up. Then he made a frown. Then, when he realized the Chico had just bitten him, Uncle Rob let out a beller like a wounded moose. Scared poor Chico so much, he chomped down on Rob's finger again. Mom went into screeching laughter and everyone from the café tried to get into the kitchen to see what was going on. By then it was too late, and they could only rely on Mom to try to tell her story, between fits of laughter, snorts and coughs. I think I remember a wheeze or two, but I was pretty young at the time.

One thing about Chico: he never forgot or forgave. I am positive that is why he is Nana's favorite. They are so much alike.

My cousins and I secretly wish there would be another Chico vs. Uncle Rob match. Mainly because we missed the first one and can only go on the accounts of the older members of our family. Mom's was the best, except she always laughed so hard it was a few years before we were able to figure out exactly what happened. Our wishes for a second round between Uncle Rob and the dog came true the night we had a particularly tasty roast beef, Yorkshire pudding and lots of gravy. Chico's favorite meal.

Wednesday, April 20, 1960
Dear Maggie:

Chico and Spotty are laying in the yard. They are happy to be home. I am sure Tippy was glad when they left. That Chico can be a pain, and he was pretty demanding on your time. He can really jump for such a little dog. For such a big tall guy, your Uncle Rob sure can jump, too! When I told Grandad about Chico and the roast, I had to stop a couple of times because I couldn't talk, I was laughing so hard. I gave a demonstration of Uncle Rob holding the Sunday roast and shaking it, with Chico hanging on for dear life off the other end. Good thing Chico had a steady grip, because when Rob swung him around the kitchen, Chico could have been hurt if he'd been shaken loose.

And you know how Chico holds a grudge against your Uncle Rob for giving him a flying lesson when Chico was such a wee pup!

We're just lucky that Chico's concentration was on the meat, or else Rob's finger would have been reminded about the biggest event in Chico's puppyhood.

Chico's reward was the big hunk of meat he managed to gulp down, all the while spinning around and around the dining room.

And with Tippy and Spotty barking like fools and you all hollering, I wish I had a camera.

Lots of the townsfolk said they missed me when I was away, because that Jehovah had his family visiting. He would have picked when I went away!

His mother and two sisters were here with a male cousin. They stayed at the Telkwa Hotel, because the Jehovah didn't want them to stay with him. I don't know why. When family visits, you put them up. Remember that, when you get older. Family is the most important thing. If family hadn't put us up, some times we would have had a hard go of things.

I think I should go find the Jehovah and tell him, but he avoids me like Uncle Rob does Chico.

Auntie Polly is wearing her wedding shoes so that they fit better when Verna gets married. They are beige. It's funny to watch her jumping between the puddles. She stops to wipe the mud off every few feet or so. She phoned me to tell me that she was leaving home with our mail. Took her twenty minutes to get here. Grandad timed her. You know that we're only a five-minute walk away.

Grandad hopes Polly doesn't get too carried away with the outfit. Next thing you know she will have Martha giving her hair advice. Martha has done it again. She's got some strange idea that orange is a color for hair. Carrots don't have a thing on Martha. We had to sit behind her one day at church, and it was hard to concentrate on Rev. Whiteside's sermon, which, by the way, was on vanity. I am sure that Martha didn't know the entire sermon was directed at her. The whole congregation was snickering.

Well, I'd best be going and put this in the mail, because Patty Phelps wants to get the bag for Terrace and Rupert to the afternoon train. I'm waiting for the bread to rise, and the walk will do me good. Might take the dogs with me, because they can use the time to sniff the town and find out what happened when they were away.

Love Nana

P.S. Tell your Mom that I have ordered four pairs of white gloves from Sears catalogue—one for you, Trudy, your Mom and Polly. And tell her that Verna wrote me and says she is getting nervous about the wedding.

Friday, April 22, 1960
Dear Maggie:

I finally tracked that Jehovah down near the Telkwa Hotel Bar. He was trying to stand near the door with his magazine, but I put him on the move with a steely gaze. I'd just come back from the Mine Road and happened to have my hunting clothes on. That might have had something to do with it, too. He dropped his magazines and was beginning to bend down to pick them up. I came close to him.

I told him that he ought to be ashamed making his family stay in a hotel. He said that's where he lives, so where else were they supposed to stay? He paid for their rooms. I guess he's been living in the back rooms above the bar since he came to town. No one wants to stay in those rooms at top dollar. It gets pretty noisy and smelly.

The Jehovah has a hot plate, and he does his own cooking and cleaning so everything works out.

I don't know why I didn't learn about this before. Everyone else in town tells me they thought I knew where he lived. I told them that it is hard for me to be protecting my property from him and be on the lookout around town to find out where he lives.

I will make a suggestion to him next time he comes to the house. There are a whole lot of sinners right below him that he might start practicing on. That way, he can stay in his yard, and I'll stay in mine.

No wonder he's usually standing between the Telkwa Hotel Bar and the Royal Bank or the Post Office. He's at his own front door.

Kind of sad, but he could move if he wants to.

Love Nana

P.S. Don't bother telling your Mother. I'm just letting you know for your own interest.

Sunday, April 24, 1960
Dear Nana:

Here is your hat. Mom has put the $20 in the ribbon. She says you weren't supposed to leave money here. If you want to put it towards things for the wedding, like gloves, etc. that is fine with her. It was fun when you were here. Thanks for all the baking. We just ate the last cookie tonight. Dad says he misses you for the cooking, but he was happy you could go home and keep Grandad hopping instead of him. I didn't see Dad hopping, other than when Chico tried to eat the roast. Annie-Lee and Robbie and I were laughing about it the other day. Uncle Rob said he should have poured gravy on Chico. Dad asked if that is because Uncle Rob is the family gravy expert, and he knows how gravy can be a showstopper. Dad says that he should have poured gravy on Uncle Rob, so he would quit swinging poor Chico around, and it was obvious that the dog was hungry.

Mom and Auntie Rene had to tell them to be quiet because they couldn't concentrate on their crib game, and we kids were having trouble counting our Monopoly money. Mom says that Uncle Rob and Dad are too much alike and that's why they argue. Uncle Rick and Trapper Art were there, too. They wisely kept their mouths full of cake.

Love, Maggie

P.S. I thought you knew that the Jehovah man lived at the Telkwa Hotel!
Patty Phelps told us about it when he moved into town.

P.P.S. Thanks for the money to buy stamps. I got twenty of them so I will have enough until the end of summer, I'll bet!

Our Home and Native Land

I just found out that some people don't like INDIANS!

My Mother plays ball with Indians, and we are friends with them. Mom says there is prejudice; just sometimes it comes in tissue and veils. Whatever that means. I know that our family is close with all the people of Telkwa. Irish, Italians, Chinese, Indian—it doesn't mean anything if your color is different. If you are an A-hole, that is another story. I have met a lot of white folk who fit the A-hole category. Way more than all the Indian people I know. My Nana and Tyee Mary are close friends. I'll bet they were both Irish in another life. More likely Nana was an Indian, as she sure can hunt and knows her way in the thickest bush. She and Tyee Mary are friends from way back. They met when they were out hunting up the Telkwa Mine Road.

They make quite the pair. Nana is close to six feet tall. Tyee Mary might be 5 feet, 2 inches tall. Tops.

Nana is slim and wiry and she has twinkly blue eyes. Nana claims that she is a champion of people first, skin color and religion second. I say maybe, except for the way she reacts to the Jehovah. Nana talks a lot.

Tyee Mary doesn't say much. She is short, stocky and round-faced. Her hands are worn out from work. She's got a thousand or more lines on her face. Mom says of lot of the wrinkles are from the triumphs and tragedies from having fifteen children and living with the same man for nearly sixty years. Tyee Mary has the best eyes. They are very large, a beautiful brown, and the corners are creased from her smiling.

I love to look at Tyee Mary because she is so colorful. She wears a headscarf, usually a bright red one. She folds her scarf low on her forehead, and snug around her head. Two braids fall to her waist.

She wears an old green or brown sweater, a blue check or purple flowered housedress and an apron that Nana made her. Tyee Mary's aprons are all colors. Her favorite is a nice pink one that Nana embroidered a little flower on. What really amazes me are her beige-colored nylons, because she wears them with grey wool work socks and work boots. And she never changes the style of her outfits, winter, spring, summer or fall.

She never trips, either. Tyee Mary's boots are always undone, and I bet they are at least four sizes too big.

For all their differences, Nana and Tyee Mary dress like twins. Except Nana wears fancy shoes with her dresses, and English boots when she goes hunting. And Nana wears nylons. Other than that, they dress exactly alike.

Old Joseph, Mary's husband, speaks less than she does. He's never learned English very well. He speaks Carrier, like his Indian Band. They belong to the Fireweed Clan. He asks Mary to interpret both English and the strange ways of some of Telkwa's folks. He is wiry and might be a bit over 5 feet 5 inches tall. I am nearly as tall as he is.

For some reason, he only wears black clothes. He wears the same hat, day in and day out. Nana says that the last thing we'll see of Old Joseph is the brim of his hat sticking up and out of his coffin.

In the late '40s, my Dad painted a picture of Tyee Mary and Old Joseph. They were heading up the Telkwa Mine Road in their horse-drawn wagon. Mary was decked out in her colorful outfit, with the evening light around her. Old Joseph was there, all in black. He is an elder with his tribal council. I love them both, because they are long-time family friends and they are really nice to me. Tyee Mary sends in smoked salmon or trout just for me, too, so I know she likes me.

Their ten sons are named after the twelve apostles. They wanted twelve boys, but had to settle for ten, so doubled up on the last two's names, and got the apostles covered that way.

One is named Matthew Judas and the other Thaddaeus James. Sounds like a first and last name for both of them. Thaddaeus just goes by T.J. because no one, even him, could spell his first name. Matthew goes by Matthew J. because people don't like calling him Judas. Not even Tyee Mary or Old Joseph. The brothers all have kids about the same ages as my cousins and me. Tyee Mary's girls have nice names, too: Little Mary, Josephine and Eve.

We just carry on with life in Telkwa and Terrace and don't give one hoot that our friends are Indians. They have a lot more respect for their friends than some people do—who shall remain unnamed at this point. But there are a few of the old biddies in Telkwa and Smithers that come to mind real quick. Mrs. Rannerfan for one. I didn't want to say her name, so I wrote it.

I've kept quiet about the Jehovah until now, and it's hard to tell everyone in town what he said to me. I know the real reason Nana doesn't like him, beside the fact that he won't look her in the eye. When we were in Telkwa at Thanksgiving, my cousins Trudy and Nan and I were sent over to Phelps & Saunders Store to get more bread and milk and a few other things. While we were there, Nana phoned over and asked Mrs. Saunders to get me to go down to the Post Office, get the mail, and then stop by the Telkwa Café, because Grandma Mulvaney had boxed up four lemon meringue pies. She said Uncle Rick was there, just finishing some apple pie, and he could give me a ride back to Nana's.

I went to get the mail. Tyee Mary was standing by the door to the Post Office. We had a quick chat and I went in to get the mail. When I came out Mary was gone. Down the street right where I had to pass was the Jehovah. I decided to say hello and be as nice as I could. After all, Nana taught us kids manners. Just because she forgot hers quite often wasn't my fault.

I was about even with him, ready to say hi, when he looked me right in the eye and said, "Indian lover."

"What in the hell is that supposed to mean?" I asked. I kind of forgot my manners, but he startled me. He must have been mad, because the hair on his head fell over and was dangling on his left shoulder as he took off and huffed his way back up the stairs and into the Telkwa Hotel.

I can't believe how long it took me to figure out what he meant. I just remembered Tyee Mary and Old Joseph are Indians.

Wedding Jitters

Saturday, May 7, 1960
Dear Maggie:

> *TWO WEEKS TO GO!*
>
> *I miss you already! Glad you're going to be here for the week before Verna's wedding. We are getting the house ship-shape, but the mud seems determined to find its way in on the feet of the dogs, and most likely Grandad. Chico has been out of sorts since I have made him stay in the kitchen. I had Grandad moving the furniture around yesterday, and he finally told me off. Guess that's a male trait. Here is some advice: find a man that lets you do what you want to do around the house. I should have known with Grandad.*

In fairness to me, I was very young and still coming into my own, when he and I wed. He's learned quite a bit, but has a ways to go in some situations, like the placement of furniture.

Had a long talk with Tyee Mary and Joseph at P & S Store yesterday. They are going to give me some oolichan grease for candles. Their son Peter came back from the Nass River Valley, where there was a great oolichan run in March.

I like the grease for a candle in the woodshed and barn.

Tyee Mary is happy to hear that your Mom will visit for a few days. She says to tell you that she saved some canned smoked salmon for you, because she knows how much you like it.

Their son John still plays men's softball and he comes to say hello when their team is in town. Peter will be away fishing again this summer. There isn't much work, and the sawmill isn't hiring Indians this year, since Mr. Rannerfan took over as mill manager. He's one to talk, with an Italian wife! The Indians are used to working in the mill, and Mr. Rannerfan should just hire them. There will be hell to pay one day.

I know— Mr. Rannerfan can hire that Jehovah and leave him behind a woodpile. Room for one of Tyee Mary's relatives to work after the Jehovah gets lost!

Grandad just came in and says to remind your Mom to bring her sheet music for the wedding march. He gave his copy to her when she was last here, and if your Mom looks carefully, she'll likely have two copies.

Love Nana

P.S. Tell your Mother about everything except my suggestion on where the Jehovah can go to work.

Ronnie's grandmother just gave us some oolichan grease candles, too. People who don't know that the Indian name for the fish is oolichan call them candle fish, because they have so much oil in them you can burn them like a candle. Every March when the oolichan run, we like to go up to the Nass River and watch the action. The Nass is an hour north of Terrace and the little fish make the river look like it's boiling. There are so many of them, it is hard to believe how small they are. Ronnie's grandmother says that the salmon and eagles eat the fish because they need the oil. Every Indian we know has oolichans on their mind the first few weeks of spring.

Monday, May 9, 1960
Dear Nana:

I saw Auntie Yvonne and Uncle Jim today. They are coming to Verna's wedding with Louis. He'll drive them in his cadilack car and he says that Verna and Ben and Jane can ride in the back seat, and Martin and I can ride in the front seat with him! I like the decorations and the horn honking the best at a wedding.

Uncle Geordie Mulvaney says he'll come to Verna's wedding, too. He's been working as a heavy-duty mechanic for Londstrom's Logging on the Queen Charlotte Islands for nearly five years now. Grandma Mulvaney was surprised he is going, because the only time she sees him is around the Telkwa Barbecue in September. We're hoping he stops here for a day or so at least, because he inherited Grandma Mulvaney's baking skills. We want some of his fresh brown bread, and a pie or two!

Love, Maggie

P.S. The Jehovah is already working, remember? If there is an extra job at the mill, maybe one of Tyee Mary's grandsons can take it. Mary's family works harder than most people I know and Mr. Rannerfan should give them a try.

Wednesday, May 11, 1960
Dear Maggie:

Here is $15. Tell your Mom to bring me these items:
    2 pair hose, size 9 ½, light beige
    1 medium-sized hairnet
    1 large bag of rice
    1 large bag of confetti
    Two boxes of pink Kleenex and one box of white Kleenex

When you receive this letter, ask your Mom to get the Kleenex right away. If you and her have time, could you start making the flowers? We need each of the boxes done, in each color, as the Cadillac is so bloody big!

We have streamers here already.

Love Nana

P.S. That should do it. Tell your Mother.

9 *PM Wednesday, May 11, 1960*
Dear Maggie:

I forgot to ask your Mom to bring her ivory handled-knife. Ours is so old it looks yellow. Polly says it won't do, as everything is in pink and white. I guess I should not have told her that Louis's car is green. She's in a snit now, and won't talk to me. Uncle Dan says that she'll start talking to me soon enough. Then I'll wish she were still in a snit. Dan nearly isn't talking to Polly, either. She is getting too bossy for her own good. I put it down to wedding jitters. Maybe because she and Dan only had the small garden wedding, and she's trying to make up for it with Verna's shindig.

Can only hope that the weather lasts. We've had nice days. Not too hot, or too cold. The lilacs are coming along fine, and Grandad is figuring out the bloom time by testing a branch by bringing it in the porch, placing it in a vase, and timing how long it takes to bloom. I'm worried for the town's lilacs. By the time he gets it right, we will have two days to go to the wedding and only enough lilacs to fill a small vase!

Love Nana

P.S. Polly just realized that the lilacs are white and PURPLE, so she asked me to tell your Mom to get some purple Kleenex, too. I haven't heard of such a thing. If you do find them, start making more flowers!

Maggie: Oh, dear. I forgot again. Tell your Mom to remember to bring her big punch bowl, the huge urn, which holds 10 gallons, and the smaller crock-pot that will hold the regular punch, and not the Rum Punch.

xo from Nana

P.S. Be sure to tell your Mother!

Friday, May 13, 1960
Dear Nana:

Mom says to tell Auntie Polly to lie down for a week and before she knows it, the wedding will be over. And Polly can go back to being her cheery self. Mom was talking to Aunt Sue last night, and they sure had a good laugh over your letter. Good thing you caught us before we left for Telkwa. In fact, I guess I should bring this letter with me because we are leaving bright and early tomorrow morning.

We are going to stop in Hazelton and pick up a bunch of things from Aunt Sue. She's going to catch a ride on the train on Tuesday, because there is something at the church on Sunday, and she can't miss it. She told Mom that she could only take four days of Polly before the wedding, so she will take her time getting there.

Love, Maggie

P.S. I am not supposed to tell you that.

P.P.S. Don't tell MY Mother!

8:30 PM Friday, May 13, 1960
Dear Nana:

Oh! I wasn't supposed to write what Mom said about Auntie Polly. Mom says that you better not have shown the letter to her, or told her about it either. She says I am as bad as you are, by just being me. I can stir the pot to boiling point almost as fast as you can, but I can't keep it simmering as long. What ever that means! Anyway, please, please, please x 100, don't tell Auntie Polly!

Love, Maggie

P.S. Tell me if you told her! I'm giving you this letter first tomorrow morning.

Saturday evening, May 14, 1960
I am leaving this on your dresser because you are here, and I was so tired I went to bed before you got back from Polly and Dan's and all the commotion.

Dear Maggie (and Fran):

What do you think I am? Crazy? One nut in town is enough, and Auntie Polly is doing just fine on her own. Grandad has read your recent letters, and wants to have a little talk with both of you when you get up tomorrow morning. Love Nana

What Are Friends For?

Nana has a good friend in Tyee Mary. She is the only other person in town that can put the Jehovah on the run. She doesn't talk to him. She's got a real talent to get him edgy.

We spent the few days before cousin Verna's wedding running all over town on errands. I was given the mail run. I had a bit of free time one afternoon, as Nana and all the aunts were having a final 'ladies' chat with Verna. Martin was off doing something and the Pike girls were at Nana's making their share of the Kleenex flowers. There wasn't anything for me to do but go sit across the street in the park while I waited for Patty Phelps to sort the mail. She told me there were a couple of parcels in the pile for Verna, and one was big. I called Mom. She told me to wait and she would send someone to pick up the parcels. And me.

Once I sat down and had a good chance to study the other side of the street, I realized that Tyee Mary was standing to the left of the Post Office door. It's the side closest to the Royal Bank and Telkwa Hotel. She was right within sight of the Jehovah, but not close enough to talk to him. He knew she was there. He'd turn his head, and she was just there, not doing anything to speak of.

The Jehovah's favorite spot to stand was between the Royal Bank and the Ladies & Gents entrance of the Telkwa Hotel Bar.

I had about an hour to kill, so got quite the show.

The Jehovah would get himself worked up now and again. He would yell at Tyee Mary to buzz off. Of course, she couldn't hear that well. She wasn't moving, anyway. Then out of nowhere, Old Joseph turned up beside Tyee Mary. They both stood still and never once glanced at the Jehovah.

It didn't take long for a small crowd to gather. A few folk saw me and came over to say hi. They asked me what I was doing. When I told him or her I was waiting for a ride, I know for a fact that each person prayed that Nana would be in the car that picked me up.

A couple of the fellows said that the men of Telkwa often spent their afternoons during the good weather sitting on the same bench. Some of them bet on whether the Jehovah would tell Tyee Mary off. They all placed bets whether it would be Nana that came to get the mail. Many people have won big on my Nana. I heard that Bobby Tarrant is really lucky. He's got extra money from his great uncle's inheritance, so he can afford to lose a bit now and again. Bobby had the sense to use the phone once in a while. He would zip over to the Telkwa Café and call Nana to say that the Jehovah was down by the Post Office and he was talking to Tyee Mary. Sometimes, Nana would bite the bait.

There were other bets, too. One I liked was how long Tyee Mary could stand without moving, and I think my favorite was how many twitches the Jehovah would make in the time Mary stood still. It required some skill to count, and the fellows often had to spell each other off, as their attention spans lost out to Tyee Mary's concentration.

The betting increased in the week before cousin Verna's wedding, because all sorts of our relatives were in town and Nana was showing off the new park by the river. It just happened to be across the street from the Post Office, the Royal Bank and the Telkwa Hotel. Not to mention the Jehovah.

After a quick look back, I knew exactly who won the bet when my Mom drove up and helped me lug the parcels into the car.

I asked Nana why Tyee Mary stands there most days and she says it is because she and Old Joseph live up by Round Lake and Mary never gets to look at the river and Hudson's Bay Mountain.

I may be young—but I'm not stupid. It's got something to do with that Jehovah. I know it.

Two Punches, You're Out

No one is sure how many people came to my cousin Verna's wedding. All I know is that Uncle Dan, who is the fire chief, said the hall could safely handle about 300. My cousins and I estimated about 300 inside and another 300 outside. Everyone was orderly and they took turns going inside for dances. That was, until Bill Buller and his Bulkley Ranchers played a rousing rendition of the Beer Barrel Polka. The music was too good to pass up. Everyone inside and outside was dancing, or at least tapping their feet to the music. Even Mrs. Grammercy, who can't hear worth a darn.

The Telkwa Hall will never be quite the same. Neither will the people. Hilda Throckmorton caught the bouquet. Uncle Rick caught the garter. They were doomed.

The townsfolk still drive by the hall and shake their heads, smile and think of the fun they had the night my cousin Verna got married.

Tuesday, May 24, 1960
Dear Maggie:

Well now, wasn't that the most beautiful wedding you have ever seen? The whole town turned out. Ben was so handsome in his uniform, and your Mom did a beautiful job on Verna's dress. The seed pearls really added to the effect.

You shouldn't have worried that your Mom forgot to wash your white socks. The blue ones from Jane looked fine. Verna was just jittery about being a bride. She didn't think you could hear her giving your Mom hell for adding blue to the color theme. Too bad that when Verna started sniffling and Auntie Polly got in on the rant, that your Mom's organ playing died right down. The sound of their voices carried into the church. It was rude of some of the men to start laughing out loud before the ceremony.

We all thought it was real cute when you walked down the aisle with no socks on. Rev. Whiteside saw you stuffing them under the pew at the back of the church. He was kind enough to return them to me after the wedding.

The Cadillac was a big hit, too! I would have liked to hear the horn more, but when it conked out on the drive back through town, everyone got a good laugh. Louis told me that you were having such fun honking before it happened. I've never seen so many cars following a wedding car. The honking was so loud that even old Mrs. Grammercy heard it. She thought they were Canada geese, and told Mrs. King that she must have missed summer because she could hear the geese.

Of course, the whole town is snickering about Martin mistaking the punches. I tried to keep a straight face when Patty Phelps was going on (and on) about Martin getting drunk. "And only a young boy," says Patty. (You should try a drink now and again, Patty!) The best part of Martin's little mistake was when he whirled young Caroline Rose round and round! Uncle Rob and Auntie Rene didn't know what hit them. Nor did Mr. & Mrs. Redfern, or the Rollings. Martha, bless her, is still complaining of a sore backside, because she tried to reach out for Mary Rollings just when Uncle Rob came flying through the air and hit her square in her big round rear with his old hard head. Good thing Martha was dancing with Trapper Art, because he caught her before she made more of a fool of herself and headed into the cake. Peter Phelps had just sprinkled 'Dance Ease' on the floor and it was just like the Telkwa Skating Rink after a good hose-down. The Good Lord was watching over Uncle Rob. He was able to go over to Grandma Mulvaney's and change out of his dress clothes with the turkey stains, and get into his comfortable clothes. The knees are gone and the rear-end is ripped clean out of his pants. Glad I had an extra safety pin on me. That pin worked and Auntie Rene's dress was as good as new. She only missed half the next dance.

I hope your Mother's head has improved by now. She and Uncle Dan and Uncle Hank had some nerve testing the punch so early in the morning. It's a miracle that Verna and Uncle Dan could make it down the aisle, him half-cut, humming 'Oh, When the Saints', and your Mother playing 'Here Comes the Bride' in polka time. Sure got the crowd going, though!

Wasn't that nice of Tyee Mary and Old Joseph and the family to come to the wedding? I was surprised to see them in full ceremonial dress. That's the first time I've ever seen all of them dressed up. They are a real handsome family. Tyee Mary made Verna and Ben each a pair of moccasin slippers.

I told the Rannerfans to keep their opinions to themselves. We didn't invite Indians to the wedding. We invited friends. I should have added that the Rannerfans were at the bottom of the list, just below the Jehovah. And he couldn't make it because Jehovah's don't sit beside Scots and Italians, like them! Just as I was thinking up things to say, the band played 'Sail Along, Silvery Moon', and I had to grab Grandad for a waltz.

Today the four remaining branches on the lilac tree blossomed. They were calling for their brother and sister branches, but those poor fellows have long since become kindling.

You left the blue socks here, Maggie. As I am positive it was no accident, and am not sure Jane wants her socks back, I put them in the Women's Institute bag for the poor. Someone ought to like the color blue. And the fact they were only worn for ten minutes.

I can hardly wait to see the pictures from the wedding!

Love Nana

P.S. Tell your Mother that your socks are lost. Martha has died her hair back to its regular sickly orange color. I think she took Polly's idea of a pink and white wedding a bit too far. I wonder what the photos will show and if her hair will come out looking as silly as it did in person. The white and pink dress was pretty, but the pink and white hat is what did it for me. She looked a bit like a pale ice cream sundae, except with a pink cherry on top! Honestly, pink hair. I have never seen anything like it. Except maybe the first time I saw her with the orange hair.

P.P.S. Tell your Mother that everyone is asking for her punch recipe. The idea of her making three extra crocks full sure went over with the crowd outside the hall.

Saturday, May 28, 1960
Dear Nana:

I showed Ronnie my bridesmaid dress with the gloves and headband, even my new white socks. I bought them at the Co-Op, with some of the money you gave me. If Ronnie and I weren't so much older now we would have liked to play 'Bride Dolls'. Just for Verna's memory, I got out both my Priscilla and Betty Bride Dolls and laid them on my bed. But I didn't play with them. Ronnie and I just tried on the bridesmaid dress a lot.

I told Ronnie's Mom and Dad about the reception and Martin's punch story. They nearly fell off their chairs laughing. Ronnie's Dad says I am going to be another Lucille Ball when I grow up, because I can tell such a funny story. I don't remember meeting Lucille. Is she someone that came from Smithers for the wedding? She doesn't live in Terrace, I know that.

Mom says thank you for asking, and her head is fine. She says any pains she has had lately are lower, and they are spelled M-O-M. She says you should read this to Grandad, because he'd get it. Mom says if she had time to write, which she doesn't, she would sign the letter Lucille Ball, because SHE is so funny. Who IS Lucille Ball?

Love, Maggie

Wednesday, June 1, 1960
Dear Maggie:

We heard from Verna and Ben. They are back in London, Ontario, after taking the train to Jasper and staying in Banff on their honeymoon. Sounds like they had a great time and are now settling into married life. Just this week, Polly had a good cry and has been fine ever since. Back to her old self.

Tell Lucille Ball that she can write or phone me some time. I have a couple of real funny things to tell HER.

Love Nana

P.S. Tell your Mother. Ask her to send the punch recipe. Everyone has named it The Telkwa Hall Rum Punch. It is already famous!

Saturday, June 4, 1960
Dear Nana:

I guess you missed it in my last letter. Who is Lucille Ball? I have no idea, and everyone keeps talking about her. I asked

Ronnie and Annie-Lee, and we know for sure that she doesn't live here.

Love, Maggie

Wednesday, June 8, 1960
Dear Maggie:

Lucille Ball is a movie actress and she has a show on TV down in Vancouver.

Love Nana

Friday, June 10, 1960
Dear Nana:

Thanks for telling me about Lucille Ball. I asked Ronnie's Dad, and he told me the day before your letter arrived.

Love, Maggie

P.S. Mom says, "Here is the famous recipe."

Telkwa Hall Rum Punch

3 bottles dark rum
1 bottle port wine
1 large can pineapple juice
1 large can orange juice
1 large bottle Lime Rickey, or 2 to taste
3 large bottles Canada Dry ginger ale
Orange, lemon and lime slices

Pour all ingredients over a large block of ice. Decorate with fruit slices. Let stand for two hours before serving.

Serves 50 people, at two drinks a person. (That is, unless my cousin, Mother and Uncles hear about your party!) This recipe can easily be doubled or tripled. (Just ask everyone in Telkwa!)

Peace in the Valley

Sunday, June 12, 1960

Dear Maggie:

Just when I was getting used to the peace and quiet, that damn Jehovah has come back to town. This time he brought a younger brother. Looks just like him—bald, but this one doesn't try to cover up his shiny round head like his brother does. This one is over-stuffed, too. Sad to say, it looks like pale watery eyes run in the family. Honestly, one of them in town was quite enough.

They were hammering on the door and I decided to throw them a curve ball. I was sweet as pie, and took their magazines and told them thank you. They thought I'd turned a corner, for sure. Once they got going on their sermon, just at the part where they were going to ask me to agree that the world was in a sorry mess and they had all the solutions, I decided I had enough. I hollered, don't you remember, I'm an Anglican? Then I reached around the door and grabbed the shotgun. I cannot repeat what I said next, but I did tell them that the best part of being an expert marksman is my reloading skills. I must say, I've missed that damn Jehovah.

Grandad hollered from the living room, so I ended up having to shut the door. Not before I chucked their magazines over the fence. That should hold them off for a while.

Love Nana

P.S. For gosh sakes, don't tell your Mother!

Tuesday, June 14, 1960
Dear Maggie:

   That damnable Jehovah! He ran right home, borrowed Patty Phelps's phone, and called Constable Reems. Would you ask your Mom to call me as soon as you read this to her?

   Tell her I might need some advice from Jack Danford if he is still a barrister. She can call me collect.

Love Nana

P.S. Be sure to tell your Mother!

Friday, June 17, 1960
Dear Nana:

   I heard Mom talking to you, then whispering to Dad. When Dad finished talking to Mom, he called Mr. Danford. Are you in trouble? I know it is that Jehovah and he is really to blame. I think I will make your best witness after Grandad. I am pretty sure you would get off if I were your witness. Dad says Mr. Danford doesn't go to court much anymore, so I hope he is willing to bail you out. It isn't all your fault!

Love, Maggie

P.S. You're not in jail are you? I figured out why that Jehovah and you don't get along. He is as stubborn as you are! Ha ha. That is supposed to make you laugh.

Tuesday, June 21, 1960
Dear Maggie:

   Thanks for your letter. Tell your Mom not to worry. Constable Reems, Jack Danford, Grandad and I have managed to settle things for now. I have been told by Constable Reems not to let anyone trespass on my property, and I can only use the shotgun when I go hunting, and then only if I use the gun five miles out of town. And the Jehovah is to STAY OUT OF OUR YARD.

That doesn't mean I don't look forward to grouse season, but that is three months away. And I look forward to seeing the Jehovah around town now and again.

Love Nana

Tuesday, June 21, 1960
Dear Nana!

Guess what!!!??? Ronnie's parents have invited me to go on holiday with them! We are going to the Okanagan and we leave as soon as school gets out. Just eight days to go!

Love, Maggie

P.S. That means I was supposed to ask you if I could come to your place in August, not July like usual. I hope I can. Uncle Rick gave me a box brownie camera and two rolls of film. He's been teaching me to take pictures, and he has a darkroom, so I can learn how to develop the photos, too. I only have one roll left because Tippy was so cute that I took a whole role of her sleeping on the heat register. Habit, says Mom, as the heat hasn't been on for a month! Anyway, I took a bunch of photos and before I knew it the roll had ended.

Mom said they will buy me a couple more rolls and will pay for the developing.

Love, Maggie.

P.P.S. Mom says I will pay for developing like I am, too. I had to get some new underwear at Fern's Specialty Shop, and it was awful, because the bra salesman was there, and Fern told Mom that she didn't think, when she told me HE could help me find my first you-know-what. I stomped out and walked all the way home. Mom brought some underwear home for me to try on, but I'm still thinking about it. Ronnie says that bras are cool, daddy-o, so she is coming over tomorrow and will help me pick two out.

I am telling you this because you can keep a secret. Not like Mom, who went and told Auntie Rene and even Mrs. Dillard! Yick!

Love, Maggie

I am starting to think like Nana. I wished that Fern and her specialty shop would leave town. That bra salesman was nice enough, but for cripes sakes, it was my first bra! Dad tried to talk to me about being stubborn. Poor Dad just didn't think things through beforehand. He suggested that the salesman was just trying to do his job, and I didn't have to be rude to him. I asked Dad if he would like Fern helping him find some nice shorts to fit his skinny arse-end. After he gave me hell for talking 'just like Nana', he told me that he could see how I might get a bit upset. Bloody right!

At Sunday dinner, I heard Dad telling Uncle Rob, Auntie Rene, Uncle Rick and Hilda Throckmorton about how I was beginning to stand up for myself. He added that it was too bad I was acting like Nana, and not the Mulvaney side of the family. Mom just had to step in, and said, "Enough about Little Nana. Hey, skinny-arse, you want some more pie?" Everyone laughed like hell, even Dad.

Uncle Rick seems to be keeping steady company with Hilda. She really has a good sense of humor. She'll need it if she wants to get in with us Mulvaneys. I like it because Uncle Rick is happy and they make a nice couple. We kids are hoping for another family wedding. We hope Martin gets to come, too. Dad says not too soon, because Mom is still drying out from Verna's wedding. I don't get it.

Saturday, June 25, 1960
Dear Maggie:

Funny you should mention her, but I was thinking of Fern and just happened to have her phone number. Tell your Mother that Fern and I had a very nice chat.

I am enclosing a note to your Mother from Fern, taped, and for her to read. Only for her to read, Maggie!

Love Nana

P.S. You decide when you want to do things. It is OK to take your time. Why, you're just twelve, and it's a month and a half before you're 13. Love again, Nana

Tuesday, June 28, 1960
Dear Nana:

Thanks for the letter from Fern. I opened it along with the letter from you, which I read after Fern's letter because I thought both letters were for me. Even if Fern says she will always help me, and she apologized for not thinking, I still don't want to go back to the store! It was way too embarrassing.

Love, Maggie

Fern should have written me, not Nana. I am NEVER, ever, buying a bra there. Ever. I did see a cute sweater in the window yesterday when Ronnie and I went by riding our bikes, and were glaring at the window. Maybe I will get Mom to stop by and see how much it costs.

Summer Holidays All 'Rand

Saturday, July 2, 1960
Dear Maggie:

When I come down in August to the doctor, you and I can go to Fern's and everything will be fine. Polly and Dan took me to the Super Value in Smithers yesterday. There are lots of nice vegetables now that summer is in full swing.

There's another ball game at the Barbecue Grounds tonight and Grandad is going to ump it.

Love Nana

Sunday, July 3, 1960
Dear Maggie:

   I hope you get this money before you leave on your holidays. It should help. The smaller amount is for you to get some things for the trip. Have a wonderful time and if you get a minute, send us a postcard.

Love Nana

Monday, July 4, 1960
Dear Maggie:

   Tell your Mother that I might need to come to Terrace for a few days, and soon. There was another slight altercation today with that Damn Jehovah. Even though I know I am in the right, there's talk around town. Probably best to leave the gossips wondering what happened, instead of telling someone who shouldn't know.

   Show this letter to your Mom. Polly says that I am acting like a crazy old lady, but as I'm only 63, she doesn't know what she is talking about. I am a young 63, at any rate. My hair is just beginning to grey. Good thing I do not take advice from Martha, and only let her style my hair instead of color it, eh?

   Tell your Mom that my train arrives on Friday at 2 p.m. and she can pick me up, or send Louis in the Cadillac. Hah hah.

Love Nana

Wednesday, July 6, 1960
Dear Nana:

   I am so excited. We leave for holidays tomorrow, and because you'll be heading to Terrace, we will just see Grandad, Chico and Spotty. Be sure to look out the train window around Hazelton. We might see each other at one of the level crossings!

   I hope you have a nice time at our place when I'm gone. I'll miss you, because I like it when you come to stay.

   I promise to write lots of postcards.

Love, Maggie

P.S. Sorry about the ripped envelope and all the scotch tape on the outside. I forgot to tell you that Mom says not to worry; she has dark paper to put over the windows the minute you get here, so no one will know you're here. She says that she thinks you might be well advised – what ever that means – to re-think a caddie ride with Louis. Dad says you might just want to get things over with and he can arrange a Patty wagon instead. I think he forgot that Patty Phelps lives in Telkwa.

Love, Maggie

Friday, July 15, 1960
Dear Nana:

Here we are in Banff. It snowed last night – in July! I got a big scare when a black bear stood up at the car window. Both Ronnie and I started screaming. So loud that Mr. Southam said his eardrums needed mending. He was kidding, because he heard us whispering in the motel room and told us to quiet down. We were talking so quietly that Ronnie and I could hardly hear each other, so that makes me believe that Mr. Southam's hearing is just fine.

We have seen about one hundred elk, 73 mountain goat and six moose, plus a whole bunch of deer of different kinds. My favorite is the mule tail deer. They sure can jump. The Southams had a good laugh when I thought they said car lots and they said mar-mots, which are sort of like a gopher that lives in the rocks. There are hundreds of them! And of course, we saw just the one bear up close. And a bunch more of its cousins, but farther away. Thank you very much other bears, for keeping to yourselves!

Tomorrow we start our visit to the States. We are going to Yellowstone Park to see Old Faithful. Hey, that's what Auntie Polly calls Uncle Dan!

Love, Maggie

P.S. I'll send you a picture of Uncle Dan. I mean, Old Faithful! Ha ha.

Tuesday, July 19, 1960
Dear Nana:

Here is a postcard of Penticton. There are two lakes, one at each end of the town. The south lake is called Skaha, and the north one is Lake Okanagan, where the famous Ogopogo lives. I didn't have time to write you from Yellowstone, but we had a good time. Old Faithful blew very high, and the Steamboat Geyser shot about 350 feet into the air. I think it is the tallest geyser in the world. The weather was hot and we only stayed there overnight. We drove nearly all the way back up the States and to Penticton in one day, and Ronnie and I fell asleep. When we woke up, we were nearly there.

We are staying in a motel right by Skaha Lake and it is sooo hot! I was able to use your money to buy two no-sleeve tops, a pair of shorts and a new bathing suit. My old one is too small since I grew up and out! Mrs. Southam went with Ronnie and me, and we tried on two-piece suits, too. Mrs. S. says that unless I am with Mom or you, I can't buy a two-piece. They are so snazzy!

Ronnie and I stayed in the motel room by ourselves last night. Mr. and Mrs. S. took a breather and went out for a nice quiet dinner. We wanted to listen to the radio and dance, but there wasn't anything on except CBC and it had the news and a bunch of loud opera music on. We ended up reading our new books. I got two Trixie Beldens and Ronnie got two Nancy Drews.

We are going to stay here for four to five days. Mrs. S.'s brother and his family arrive tomorrow; we will all have a nice visit.

Love, Maggie

Sunday, July 24, 1960
Dear Nana:

I'm writing this in the car on the way home. We had so much fun with the Franklins, especially Rusty Franklin. He is very tall and is nice to us. Rusty is nearly 17!!!! The twins, Sandra and Diana, are nearly 14. We rented a boat, and the only one who could water ski is Rusty. He is so nice. He's going to write me when he gets back to Vancouver. Rusty is really very nice, too. He kind of reminds me of Trapper Art.

Love, Maggie

Monday, July 25, 1960
Dear Maggie:

It was good to see you and Ronnie and family. Sorry you couldn't stay for dinner, but I know that Mr. Southam wanted to get on to Terrace. It is always that last three hours of the trip that make you want to push on towards home.

You have a pretty tan, except for the burnt nose. You have to watch that, and not burn yourself. Wear a hat. We have a good garden this year, so when you come up next week, remember to bring your old shoes for working in the patch. Grandma Mulvaney will have a lot of the Mulvaney kids there so you can play together. Remember that Jane and Trudy will be here for part of the time, so you and Martin will have many things to do, including visiting with your cousins. Grandad was in the barn yesterday and he found a few things that you kids might like to see.

We will go to the lake for a picnic one day. You can help me with the canning for the Bulkley Valley Fall Fair. I think my pickling cucumbers for dills are very good this year, and I've already put up the raspberry jam.

Martha was by yesterday and I am not sure what happened. She has to wear a scarf, even in the shop. She had a bit of a disagreement with a color jar. Her older sister Becky is visiting and says that there are a few chunks missing out of the back of her head. I think she meant chunks of her hair, although those two never did get along real well. Speaking of Martha. She and Trapper Art seem to be starting something. A lot of people in town have seen them walking by the river, or sitting on the same side of the booth at the Telkwa Café. He is colorblind. Did you know? So maybe that's why he can see past Martha's hair-do and see her for the pretty young woman that she is. We'll keep you posted!

We had a meeting with Tyee Mary's sons, mostly about the Telkwa Barbecue. Mr. King won't be in town this year, so we will help oversee the beef. Tyee Mary's sons say that they will help Grandad. Your Mom and

Dad, Uncle Dan, Ben and Mary Rollings, and Vern Hopkins will help, too. Grandad says that if we get six to eight hindquarters for the pit, we should be in good shape. I say, make it ten, because I love the flavour and could easily eat a side myself! Tell your Mother that she is to help.

You will have to stay overnight with me when your Grandad, Mom and Dad tend to the fire. They won't be home until late, as the beef goes in around 1 a.m. Sure is worth the wait, though. Remember not to eat any Cheezies or drink orange pop until after you've had a couple of sandwiches. Ha.

Love Nana

P.S. Tell your Mother to bring her ball gear, as the ladies are hoping she'll come back to play a game or two with the Telkwa Ramblers.

I can't believe that Trapper Art would be interested in Martha Throckmorton. She's OK, but he needs a younger wife. Martha is probably as old as he is. He better not marry her.

Swimming Lessons

For the first part of August, we went with Uncle Rob and Auntie Rene, Robbie and Annie-Lee to a cabin at Lakelse Lake, which is about ten miles out of Terrace. You drive past the Airport turn off and then go down the big hill, which is called Airport Hill. (I wonder why? ha ha.) Then you make a sharp right turn just at the end of the straight stretch, which always scares the hell out of our mothers, because by the time the turn comes, the car and our Dads are enjoying the speed.

We have the use of the cabin for as long as we want, and all we have to do is keep it clean, and make sure that it is locked. We don't have to pay rent. But the cabin needs some help, and so for the first week we are on a work bee, and are painting and cleaning up and the men are clearing bush "for things," says Dad. The men seem to enjoy making a big pile of trees and crap, and now they are trying to figure out where to put the stuff so that they can actually use the clearing they made. For what, we aren't sure. Anyway, they are having as much fun as us kids, so it seems like a holiday to them.

Mom and Rene and all the cousins are staying for two weeks after Dad and Uncle Rob finish their ten days mucking around, and have to go back to town to work. They will come out on Fridays and stay till early Monday mornings.

The Island and Williams Creek were used as a fishery testing spot. The creek is one of the fastest flowing in our area, and the island was made when the water decided to take a second route out to Lakelse Lake, says Uncle Rick. The cabin is at one end of the island, and is about a five-minute walk through the bush to a sandy beach on the shore of the lake. Annie-Lee and I tried to take a walk in the creek the day we arrived. We were neck deep in a second, and had to swim like hell to keep from going under. We were half way to the lake—about 200 yards—before we could grab hold of some branches and pull ourselves to shore.

Uncle Rick and his fiancée Hilda came out for the first weekend. He and Dad rigged up a pulley system across the widest part of the creek. We go in the old rowboat at the roadside landing, and fifty feet down, we make it to the other side, right by our cabin. Then we have to lift up a wet rope and everyone pulls hand over hand to send the boat back to the roadside.

Annie-Lee and I are pretty weak, so looks like we won't have to do the pulling back till we're older. Hilda got out of it, too. She's got a big diamond on her finger and was worried about losing it in the water. Uncle Rick told her to keep her damn hands clasped and sit on them if she had to. He says he's not about to do any underwater mining for a diamond ring, because he had to do a lot of regular mining for copper and gold to get her the ring in the first place. Annie-Lee, Robbie and I spent a bit of time trying to clasp our hands and sit on them, until Mom told us to sit still or start swimming.

We were doing fine. As long as we kids stayed still, we were allowed to go back and forth with the Uncles, bringing all our stuff across. That was until we hit a wave and the boat lurched. Robbie got it in the face with a tree branch. He stood up. Over he went. Next thing you know his black head is bobbing along, all the way to the lake. He came back on the trail from the beach about fifteen minutes later. That was his favorite thing to do for the rest of the week. Except getting hit by a tree branch.

Whenever Uncle Rick and Dad get together, they start inventing things. Since he had just rigged up a successful boat pulley, Dad was in the mood to invent. He wanted to hook up another pulley. There was a steep bank to a small wooden platform, behind the cabin. That's where you were supposed to get water, which was high from the late June and early July rains. The platform was about a foot under water. Not too safe, says Dad. Uncle Rob nearly fell in head first, trying to prove the point that if you held on to a tree limb, it would be O.K. and even us kids could get a little bucket full if we were careful.

We were glad to have been there for the demonstration. Uncle Rob grabbed hold of the branch just as a gush of water hit his feet. He swung around so fast his bum dipped into the icy water when the branch started to give way. Thank gosh Uncle Rob has quick reflexes, and he did us all proud. His feet ran up the bank before the rest of his body, and he landed between Robbie and me.

Right after that, the pen and paper came out and the inventing really picked up speed.

Dad thought that if they tied a bucket to a rope on a pulley, they could lower it into the creek and then bring a fresh bucket back to the kitchen window. Then Mom and Auntie Rene could have lots of water for cooking and washing. The main reason was because when the water ran out and we kids were at the beach and not able to help, our Dads and Uncle Rick had to go get the water. The men wanted their wives to have a bit of a holiday, too. Right after they did the dishes.

Mom put a stop to us kids going near the creek, because the bank wasn't too safe, either. I suggested that they might try to build another platform, a couple of feet higher, with sides on it, so we could go help, but no one listened to me. Then I thought about it, and decided it was more fun to play at the beach and didn't invent one more thing during our whole stay.

All three of the brothers spent most of our first Saturday drawing out the plan. We had a wiener roast for supper. Uncle Rob put some wood on the fire from the big pile of brush they cleared earlier in the day. We were all sitting around waiting for some good coals so we could roast marshmallows.

Dad never can sit still. He said he was going to go over and pace off the length from the creek to the cabin. Uncle Rick and Rob said, "Suit yourself." We watched Dad wandering back and forth in the tall grass behind the cabin. Dad is six feet tall, and the grass came up to his chest.

All of a sudden, Dad disappeared. It looked like someone or something yanked him into the ground. Annie-Lee, Auntie Rene, Hilda, Mom and I saw it happen. "A.E.!" Nothing. We stood up. "Dad!" "A.E.!" Mom was up, with Annie-Lee and me right behind her. The rest of the family turned around just in time.

As quick as he had gone out of sight, Dad popped back up. He had a look of terror on his face. And a piece of toilet paper on his head.

"CESSPOOL! Jesus Christ! The cesspool!" Poor Dad. He was covered from head to toe in green and brown crap. With a toilet paper bonnet, added Uncle Rick.

Dad ran like a fool to the boat landing. He flew into the creek. He doesn't swim too well at the best of times. Maybe the poo weighted him down a bit. Last we saw of him was his brown and green head, topped with a white headpiece, travelling in the same direction Robbie had taken earlier in the day.

The sad thing is that Dad had to walk back to the cabin without one of us coming to see if he was O.K. We were on the ground, rolling around in hysterics. I think Dad was really hurt that none of us asked him how he was. Once he came within smelling distance, we started to go towards him, then thought better. We all ran to the porch. Mom went inside the cabin and came out with a bucket, a scrub brush and some soap. Uncle Rick didn't help him much by saying, "Too bad we haven't had the chance to hook up the pulley system. Looks like you'll need a few buckets worth."

Monday, August 22, 1960
Dear Nana:

Thanks for the card and the money for my birthday. I love the new bra. Good thing you made sure that the outside of the package was marked that it was to be opened only by me, in my room! Ronnie told me I had to make sure I wore it when we go to the circus this weekend. *Wagner's Shows are here until the weekend, go to Rupert after that, then they move to Hazelton mid-week and end up in Smithers for the Fall Fair.*

I heard Mom on the phone with you, telling the story of Dad and the cesspool. Gee, was that funny. Poor Dad! He is bruised all over from whacking against the branches when he rode out to the lake. It's been nearly three weeks, too! One thing he says he'll do is take swimming lessons. Mom told him he'd be better off getting new glasses. Everyone was surprised that there had been a toilet in that area of the island. Dad and Uncle Rick drew a map the island after the 'poo-incident' as Mom called it, and they figured out a use for all the spare brush and stuff and made a big fence around the cesspool hole. Gave them something to do. Uncle Rob refused to help. He said if he wanted to go near a cesspool, he'd just sit next to Dad.

Love, Maggie

P.S. Be sure to tell Uncle Dan, Auntie Polly and Martin. I know they'll get a bang out of this one!

Johnny Destiny:
Big Shot of the Telkwa Barbecue

Thursday, August 25, 1960
Dear Nana:

Hello from the Mulvaney softball training camp!
Now that we're back from holidays, Mom has already heard from Mary Rollings and Daisy Pahat. She has had me pitching balls

to her all week! I get on my bike to go pick them up, because she hits them so far. I think she should go into the World Series, because by my figuring, Mom can hit as far as Mickey Mantle any day. Then we could listen to her games on CBC radio when the World Series is on. Mom has already marked off any outside engagements from October 5 onwards to make sure she isn't doing a thing during the World Series. You know what that means for me. I have to help add up the scores and figure out the averages. Mom says it's good for my mathematical ability. Dad says Mom just doesn't believe some of the scores and she needs a second opinion.

I got a letter from Ronnie's cousin, Rusty Franklin! He is so nice. He told me that he thought I was a very nice young girl and that I should work hard in school. He is quitting school soon and going to try to join the Air Force. When he comes for a visit next summer, he'll wear a uniform. Just like the Mounties, except a navy color.

Mom says to get it in my head now that I can't go out with him unless Ronnie is around and her older sister Wendy is there. I don't see why. Dad says that jailbait never figures out until it's in the trap. What do you make of that? Dad says to ask Mom, and Mom said she would tell me, but only after she hears what YOU have to say on the subject. What the heck are you guys talking about? I just don't get it. Dad says I'd better not get it. Help!

Love, Maggie

P.S. Say hi to Grandad and Uncle Dan, Auntie Polly and Martin for me. What do you hear from the Pikes? I guess you heard about Uncle Rick and Hilda Throckmorton. He popped the question on her birthday, just a few days before we went to the cabin. I heard him talking to Mom and Dad and he was asking them to stand up for him, or something.

Monday, August 29, 1960
Dear Maggie:

This should reach you just before you leave for the Telkwa Barbecue.

When your Mom and Dad are talking about jailbait, they mean to give you a compliment. You are a nice young girl, and we all look forward to keeping you that way. See you soon.

Love Nana

P.S. Be sure to tell your Mother

8 p.m., September 5, 1960
Dear Nana:

Thanks for the great time at the Telkwa Barbecue. I sure had fun. Johnny Destiny was the best thing about the whole weekend.

Too bad that dang Jehovah walked by just as you were playing the ring toss. I am positive that you would have won something, if it were not for him making you spin around a time or two extra.

Mr. Thomas at the garage took the dint out of the car roof. Dad told Mom not to park the car behind the backstop. Actually, it was just right of the backstop. We could see better if we were tired of sitting on the bleachers and wanted a soft seat to enjoy while watching Mom pop her home runs. Who would have thought that Mom's only fly ball would have made such a clunk? Good thing Grandma Mulvaney was dozing in the back seat. Dad says he saw her jump up so fast, if she had been in the front, she'd likely have gone through the window! Both he and Uncle Rob were trying not to laugh when they offered to drive Grandma home to change her pants. She didn't think it was that funny and told them a thing or two. More like a thing or four. She told all us Mulvaney kids that she hopes our mothers have better manners, so we will at least learn something. She wondered where she went wrong with all her boys. Mom and Auntie Rene were happy to tell her. Uncle Rick stepped in and broke it up. Mom says it is because Grandma Mulvaney has a bit of English mixed in with her Irish that she didn't laugh like hell!

Love, Maggie

I still go into hysterics about Johnny Williams riding the horse. Nana missed it, because she was over by the horseshoe pitch watching Grandad win.

Johnny has always been scared of horses. His wife Marg is such a good horsewoman, so he thought he'd show her he could ride. Dad says that the Strange boys shouldn't have given him such a high-spirited horse. We all thought he'd do OK because he was in the corral. When the horse trotted to the end of the corral, it looked like everything was going fine. Johnny turned its head too quickly. When the poor horse felt Johnny loose his balance and accidentally kick its side, the thing took off as if it was at a racecourse or had the Devil chasing it, or both. I am sure it would have stopped, but we'll never know because about three-quarters of the way along, Johnny dove off that horse just like he does at the lake. Except neither the dock or the diving board are ever travelling at a full gallop. Too bad about the dirt being there and not water. Mom says that from her and Hilda's vantage point in the stands, he should have gotten some sort of award for diving, if not for horse riding.

Poor Johnny! He looked so sad! Marg and Uncle Rick and Dad told him to clean himself up, and get back up on the horse. Johnny took a bit of coaxing. So did the horse, come to think of it. Johnny is such a little guy, so after about five minutes of him saying "no," two of the Strange boys just flung him back on the horse. The horse started to walk slowly forward, and it looked like both horse and rider were eyeing each other up.

Johnny was going to have no nonsense from this horse. It was when he pulled the reigns so tight, that the horse took a walk all on its own. Backwards. Johnny was hollering, "Get me off this F- - - - - -g horse! Make it stop doing that!" Marg kept real calm and said, "Let go of the reigns, Johnny. Johnny, let go of the reigns." He kept yelling, "Make it stop!"

By the time everyone stopped laughing, got up from the ground and dusted off, Johnny and the horse were nearly back to their starting point at the other end of the corral. Johnny looked pretty mad when one of the Strange boys rode in and lifted him off the horse, and plopped him down in front of Marg.

We saw him about an hour later, after the Mulvaney brothers and Strange boys had bought him a couple beers and a beef sandwich to make up for it. I still laugh out loud once in a while when I think of it.

The horse's name is Destiny. Now everyone in town calls him "Johnny Destiny." I still call him Johnny, because it isn't nice to tease people too much. It sure was funny, though.

September 7, 1960
Dear Maggie:

As I'll be down there in a couple of days, and you'll need more than one bra, I'd be happy to pay a visit with you to Fern and her specialty shop.

Grandad and I agree with you. Johnny Destiny was surely the highlight of the Telkwa Barbecue. Followed very closely with Grandma Mulvaney and the 'sky is falling.'

Tell your Mother that she is the talk of the town for pulling in the winning home run, especially with the bases loaded.

The house is quiet now that you kids are back home. We had lots of fun this summer. Thanks again for being such a help in the garden and kitchen. When the Bulkley Valley Fall Fair is on in Smithers, we'll show them just who can make pickles, won't we? I entered both you and me, as there are a few categories. We can talk about the Fair when I am down there. Grandma Mulvaney is entering her famous lemon meringue pies, and Auntie Polly has some jams, jellies and her crocheting entered. Uncle Dan says that it's too bad there isn't a category for best party of the year, because Verna's wedding would take the cake! We should get your Mom's punch recipe entered. Patty Phelps is a judge.

See you soon.

Love Nana

P.S. Tell your Mother and Father that I heard through the grapevine that Johnny Destiny is giving swimming lessons, now that he is an expert from diving off his horse. Might work for your Dad if he comes across any more cesspools next time he's out in the bush.

September 9, 1960
Dear Nana and Grandad:

I have spent some of the money you gave me for my birthday. Thanks again! I went to the Hub newsstand and got a movie *magazine and some candy with just a bit of the money, and I was going to buy stamps but Mom and Dad gave me new ink, paper, envelopes and stamps, so I'm set! One-half of the money went to savings and the rest I am going to use for new outfits for school. Because I am going into high school this year, I will need some new clothes. And I've grown so much this year; nothing fits very well from last year. Mom wants me to go back to Fern's Specialty Shop for a bigger bra, but I don't want to go until you can come with us.*

Love, Maggie

P.S. Thanks again, Nana. I have prayed that the bra sales MAN is there when you come to town. I am positive he would enjoy meeting you.

I got another letter from Rusty Franklin. He says he cannot write me any more because his steady girlfriend found my letters, and gave him you-know-what supreme. I would have liked to see him in his Air Force uniform, but he was just a childhood crush, anyway.

In Eddie Charlie's Memory

Wednesday, September 14, 1960
Dear Maggie:

What a commotion is going on in town. Martin got a heck of a surprise last night when Uncle Dan took him to the regular Tuesday night fire practice.

The Telkwa Volunteer Fire Department takes its work seriously. They built a little shack the week before, just beside the fire hall. This fire practice, they lit it on fire and were letting it get a good bunch of flames on it, before they started the fire truck and the officers jumped on for the fifty-foot ride.

You know that big reservoir on top of the fire hall that used to be for the town's drinking supply? Martin was up on the first level, safe and out of the way. He couldn't see the firemen because of the smoke and flames, so he decided to climb the tall ladder. He was half way around the walkway when something in the reservoir caught his eye.

It looked like a black mop, moving in the breeze off the Bulkley River. Martin watched the mop for a few seconds, and then realized there was something attached to it.

Turns out, it was Eddie Charlie. He'd been gone a few days. He does that now and again, so no one was worried about him.

Uncle Dan says Martin was calm, and hollered down to the firemen that they might think twice before they took a drink from the fire hose.

Mr. Redfern and Uncle Dan climbed up to see what Martin was going on about, and there was poor old Eddie.

Took the fire department a while to rig up their ladders to be able to hoist him out, and down to the ground. Then they had to wait until the coroner arrived from Smithers, along with Constable Reems.

Joe Charlie was the last to see his brother Eddie alive. Joe Charlie isn't too good knowing or remembering his days of the week. Uncle Dan says that when Constable Reems was making his report, Joe had a hell of a time.

Constable Reems asked when Joe last saw Eddie.

Joe says Wednesday the 14th.

Wednesday, the 14th?

Yep, says Joe.

Constable Reems looked at the calendar and said it isn't the 14th until tomorrow.

Why not? says Joe.

Because today is only the 13ᵗʰ.

What day is today? says Joe.

Today is Tuesday.

OK says Joe. Tuesday.

You say your brother alive this Tuesday or last Tuesday?

"Yep," says Joe. "Not counting Sunday the 4th. We had a beer behind the Telkwa Hotel Bar. It was closed, so it must have been Sunday."

Uncle Dan had to turn away because he was trying to keep a straight face. (Remember, Maggie. Death is not a laughing matter.) Then Mr.

Redfern said he'd last seen Eddie by Phelps & Saunders store about Friday or maybe Saturday. Constable Reems started to ask him which day, and Uncle Dan stepped in and said that maybe it was best to call it a day, and the fact that Eddie Charlie is dead and Joe and maybe Mr. Redfern were the last two people to see him alive might be about all that Constable Reems can hope for.

We heard that poor Constable Reems decided to write up his report and put in the date of death as unknown. That's three of the Charlie brothers who are gone from here. Pete and Eddie died. And Phillip Charlie, but he just moved to Terrace.

No one knows what happened, other than everyone agrees that Eddie fell in the reservoir. Constable Reems says that he won't bother with an investigation.

Martin is OK. He only saw the back of Eddie's head, so he is not too upset.

The Telkwa firemen are having a meeting this week to decide whether to drain the reservoir or use the water when they put out the fires around town. They would just tell folks it is in memory of Eddie Charlie. I remember Eddie swimming in the river near there when he was a kid, so I am sure he wouldn't mind helping out the Telkwa Fire Department.

It is fitting that Eddie Charlie died at the Fire Hall. He loved watching fire practice, and could always be counted on to lend a hand, or say something funny about what the men were doing. He was a happy guy, and was no trouble to anyone in town. Except to the water supply.

I thought we could have a work bee and clean out the reservoir, but your Uncle Dan says that the Fire Department will drain the reservoir and then put the big fire hose to work, cleaning out the whole thing. We're hoping for some rain while the cleaning goes on, because it'll take a couple days to drain, clean, and put the water back.

I'll bet that Damn Jehovah is relieved. Eddie Charlie liked to stand by Tyee Mary when she spent time by the Post Office. He was as chatty as Mary is quiet. Eddie was able to break the Jehovah's concentration, which drove the Jehovah to take up hollering. I am sorry I missed that, as I only just heard about it from Bobby Tarrant.

Eddie's funeral is this Saturday. Grandad and I are going. He's to be buried on the reserve next to his Mom and Dad and brother Pete.

Love Nana

P.S. Tell your Mother

Just Strummin' Along

Sunday, September 18, 1960
Dear Nana:

Guess What??? Patty Phelps visited us and I heard her telling Mom about two of the Telkwa Ramblers ball players who got in a fight at the Ladies & Gents side of the Telkwa Hotel Bar. Wilma Carp and Julie Bristle were arguing about MOM! They went for beers after the Telkwa Ramblers last game of the season, just before the Bulkley Valley Fall Fair Dance.

As usual, they were sitting on opposite sides of the bar. Wilma just can't forgive Julie for kissing Bill Carp when they were 12.

Wilma said Mom was lucky to have hit the home run at the Barbecue, and Julie told Wilma that she didn't know what in the H. she was talking about—everyone knows that Mom is the best ball player in the whole damn Northwest. Julie also reminded Wilma that she could have been a good ball player, too, if she didn't drink so much beer and have to be peeing at the outhouse every time the Ramblers are up to bat.

Patty says that at first they were just hollering across the bar. Then Julie delicately strummed her guitar, which she'd brought in from her car. Wilma had a couple more beer. Julie commenced to play a song that rubbed Wilma the wrong way. She shrieked, at the top of her lungs, "I don't like that song!"

When Wilma screeched, Julie stopped strumming her guitar and slowly put it down. She stood up and walked over to where Wilma was sitting, all the way across the beer parlor. Wilma rose slowly, and was ready for their little chat.

Julie didn't give Wilma much chatting time. She reached out and put her whole hand in Wilma's cleavage, and ripped her Telkwa Ramblers shirt AND her bra right off! Then Julie walked back towards her chair, dropped Wilma's shirt and bra into Peter Phelps's lap, headed back to her chair, picked up her guitar, and strummed the same song.

"This is Wilma's favorite."

Patty says that everyone knew Wilma Carp was built, but they had no idea just how well. Patty says no wonder that Bill Carp wants to go home with her every night when the bar closes.

I guess what happened next should have been expected. Wilma wandered over towards Julie, who kept busy strumming her guitar. She stopped by Peter Phelps, whose mouth was still wide open. Wilma bent over, closed Peter's mouth, and picked up what was left of her shirt. She put it on and did up the bottom button, which Patty says was the only one left.

Wilma slowly and carefully reached out, picked up a fresh pitcher of beer from Peter's table and marched right over to Julie. She lifted the pitcher high as she could and poured it on Julie's head. The cold beer loosened her grip on the guitar. Wilma grabbed the guitar neck out of Julie's hand, hauled off and broke the whole guitar over her head.

"I told you I didn't like that God-damned song!"

I couldn't hear everything that Patty said after that because she and Mom were laughing so hard that Tippy barked.

I thought you would like to hear Patty's version, just to see how well it matches with the rest of Telkwa's version.

Love, Maggie

P.S. DON'T tell Mom! She doesn't know I was listening.

Tuesday, September 20, 1960
Dear Maggie:

This is the only time I will tell you: It is very rude to report things you overhear. I think it is best to just overhear them and not repeat them, especially in writing.

However, that is pretty well the same story I've heard more than enough times in the past few days.

We're sending you this money to say congratulations on your big win at the Bulkley Valley Fall Fair. Both Grandad and I are very proud of you.

Ever since you were a little girl, you've loved pickles, so you might think about a job in the future as Pickle Queen or something like that!

The idea you had of adding five cloves of garlic and the chilli pepper was a good one. That is surely what won you the prize.

Patty Phelps has been asking for the recipe. I told her it is a family secret; so when she calls, and I know she will, don't tell her!

Love Nana

P.S. Tell your Mother that Auntie Polly won for her crocheted pillowcase, and Grandma Mulvaney picked up the Grand Prize for her Lemon Meringue Pie.

The other reason that I won the prize is because I was the only kid entered in the pickles category.

Thursday, September 22, 1960.
Dear Nana and Grandad:

Thanks for the money! I sure didn't expect to get more money so soon after my birthday. Then you sent me the money for school, and now this. Thanks! I am going to put half in savings (Mom says) and then get another outfit at Fern's or some new shoes and a jacket from Sears Catalogue. I hope this reaches you before you come down. Mom left her famous bat by the outhouse the day we left, and just remembered it today. Dad says there is so much manure around that area of your yard that you had better check to see if it has rooted before you grab it and take it inside.

Anyway, we hope you can bring it with you because Mom is still playing ball once in a while, and she wants her lucky bat. You know that the World Series starts soon and she'll have to be out at least once or twice a day, recreating the hits of her favorite players.

Love, Maggie

P.S. Mom says she doesn't want to be hearing about the bat from Auntie Polly or Aunt Sue. She says to make sure you get right on the train, and not go looking for that poor Jehovah just because you happen to have a bat handy. Dad says that there will be two bats travelling to Terrace. Did someone else forget theirs?

P.P.S. Mom says TELL GRANDAD WHAT SHE SAID. She hollered it and told me to print it in capital letters!

Saturday, October 1, 1960 (The day before my birthday!)
Dear Maggie:

I sure enjoyed visiting you folks! That was the quietest time I think we have ever had together. The early snowstorm was something, wasn't it? I am sorry we didn't get to Fern's Specialty Shop. I think you will have no problems when you go in there, though. Fern and I had a good talk on the phone.

There was some bad news when I got home. The Stoddard's house burned down. It was just like Grandma Mulvaney's when her house at the lake went up in '57. No one was home, and they don't know what caused the fire. When young John Stoddard was getting off the bus from school, he could smell smoke. Just then, the whole place went up in flames. Wee Mary Rollings only lives a quarter mile down the road, and she said it sounded like the bombs in London during the war.

The Stoddards lost everything, so if you have some clothes for the two girls and your Mom and Dad can send something along for Mr. & Mrs. Stoddard, that would be a big help. The whole town has pitched in, and Patty Phelps says she and Peter are thinking about going to the south for the winter, so she is lending the Stoddards her place until March or April. I know damn well that Patty Phelps hates going South and she loves the winters here because she tells me that each year. She IS English, and so are the Stoddards, so my guess is that Patty is getting soft in her old age. Her husband Peter will have something to say about where they spend the winter.

We are adding a raffle for the Stoddards at the Women's Institute Thanksgiving Tea. Tell your Mother that I have bought her a couple tickets, as one of the prizes is a sweater set from Fern's, courtesy of her sister, Daisy Pahat.

The firemen and fellows from the John Deere Tractor Company where Mr. Stoddard works have gone around town collecting furniture and clothing.

Monday, October 3, 1960

Well, back to finish this. The Women's Institute ladies came by with a cake for me on the 1st, as my birthday fell on Sunday and we were all busy with church and family dinners. Polly and Dan invited us to their place for roast beef and all the trimmings on Sunday. Thanks for the phone call.

Now I hear that Patty Phelps has arranged for the old Thenhorne place to be fixed up and it will go to the Stoddards. I knew she wouldn't leave town! She was being kind, and doing something nice for those less fortunate than she is. That is something for you to remember, Maggie. Always do something kind for others, and treat them as you would like to be treated.

Grandad and I have gathered up as many household goods as we can, and we took part our of pension cheque this month and had it made into cash. I borrowed Martin to write the Stoddard's name on the envelope, and he dropped it off at the post office. They don't need to know where the $25 came from. I don't care if they ever find out. You and your Mulvaney cousins might want to take a bit from your allowances and mail something to each of the kids. I don't think the kids have any spending money.

Love Nana

P.S. Tell your Mother to let Auntie Rene and Uncle Rob know about the Stoddards.

P.S. Don't tell your Mother this: Mr. Redfern and Bobby Tarrant were by to see Grandad today. They dropped an envelope off for him. Bobby told me that I would be happy to know that Tyee Mary has taken to guarding the Jehovah for me. I asked him why he thought I'd be happy about that. He didn't really know what to say. I said that maybe it's because they're losing some money on me lately, and wanted me to go see for myself. I really have been too busy to go to the Post Office or the bank this past while, what with being in Terrace and getting organized for the Thanksgiving Tea. It's just a week away!

Anyway, I told Bobby that he'd best 'fess up, because I know that his informant gives him a call once in a while, just to let him know that I'm leaving the house on errands. Grandad's face got all red. Hah! I knew he had placed a bet on me, too. My own husband. I fixed him. Opened the envelope and took out $5 for Grandad's troubles, then went over and got a new envelope and put the money in it and printed 'The Stoddards' on the outside. Taped it real good and handed it to a very surprised Bobby Tarrant.

Love Nana

P.S. to my P.S. Don't tell your Mother. She'll just get mad at her Dad, and we don't need that. I thought that you might like to know that more than one person in town is watching out for me. And we're all watching out for the Stoddards.

The Telkwa Fire Department held a big square dance for the Stoddard's at Alice and Bobby Tarrant's place. Mom and Dad drove up for it. They raised enough money to help the family to buy some appliances for when they begin to rebuild their house next spring.

I had a good talk with Nana when she visited us. I knew damn well that Tyee Mary would NEVER have gone and stood by the Jehovah if Nana hadn't put her up to it. She made a deal with Tyee Mary. Mary didn't have a lot to do some days. She liked the chance to come into town. It didn't bother her if the Jehovah said things to her, because she couldn't hear that well anyway. Here's this old lady, standing just like the Jehovah. So still, you couldn't tell if she was breathing. Except I could. The twinkle in her eyes gave it all away. She was having a lot of fun, and she was driving the poor Jehovah crazy. All on behalf of her friend, Nana Noonan.

I told Nana she should start betting on when the Jehovah was going to holler at her and split the money with Tyee Mary. Then they could half it again and give some to the Stoddards. Sort of like what Mom and Dad make me do whenever I get money given to me. I can spend a little bit and the rest gets taken away from me faster than I can count it. Mom says it is for my education and for a rainy day. That's a good one. It rains here more than anywhere else in the Pacific Northwest. I want my money!

Lemon Moose

I got a letter from Martin about Eddie Charlie. He says he wasn't even scared. Just interested. Sure would have scared me! I do not want to see dead people. EVER!

Uncle Rick told us he nearly got a chance to be dead over the weekend. Good thing he didn't because he and Hilda have their wedding date set for next spring.

He was delivering some supplies to Trapper Art, who has taken on the job as a forest fire ranger and general caretaker of Malkow Lookout. Trapper Art likes the peace and quiet, and hopes he can get on regular with the Forest Service. Dad got him the job. I think Trapper Art needs a wife, and it better not be that Martha "Funny-Hair" Throckmorton. It's mainly because I'm not available yet, that I hope he can stay up at Malkow Lookout for a few years. I've told Nana to keep him in mind, when she is going around town with her "Cupid's Bow," her trusty 410 shotgun! Nana says she thinks Trapper Art is doing OK on his own. She says that he seems to have taken a real shine to Martha.

Fall is setting in but it's been really hot. The Forest Fire watch is going longer than everyone thought. Trapper Art radioed down to the Ranger Station in Telkwa that he needs a few more things to get him through the extra two or three weeks before he closes the lookout for the winter. He had a long list of things. He added a box of Coca-Cola at the end.

Uncle Rick happened to drop by the Ranger Station to say hello to Ben Rollings, who just got promoted to Assistant Ranger. Malkow Lookout is on the way back to where Uncle Rick has been prospecting, and he hadn't seen Trapper Art all summer. He volunteered to drive his trusty Land

Rover up the mountain to Malkow Lookout and stay overnight so he could have a nice visit with Trapper Art.

Things went pretty well at the Super Value in Smithers. Uncle Rick picked up everything on Trapper Art's list, including his box of Coke.

He even stopped by the Telkwa Café on his way to the Lookout and picked up one of Grandma Mulvaney's lemon meringue pies from Auntie Meryl.

He made good time, and once he took the turn-off to the Lookout, he was bouncing along nicely, making his way to Trapper Art.

Coming around the last bend in the road, right where it gets really steep, and just before you gun the car to get it to chug up the last rocky part before the Lookout, a moose hopped up from the side of the road.

"There's not much space on either side," says Dad.

He and Uncle Rick wasted time in the story trying to figure out the size of a moose.

Mom said, "It's big. Now get on with your story, Rick."

Uncle Rick says he stopped his Land Rover. Quickly.

He rolled the left window down and hollered to the moose to move its arse. He's Dad's brother, though it sounds to me like he has spent some time with Nana lately, saying something like that.

I guess the moose didn't understand English. It stomped towards the Land Rover—and Uncle Rick, the lemon meringue pie and Trapper Art's Coke.

It just kept coming, until its knees were at the grill. Its head was hung over the hood, and its nose was on the windshield.

Uncle Rick decided to honk the horn. Honk. Honk. Nothing. Except that the moose moved a bit closer and gave the Land Rover a nudge.

The Land Rover and Uncle Rick moved back a few inches. The engine was still running so Uncle Rick revved the engine and really honked the horn.

He's not sure what happened first. Or second. But he knows what happened third.

The moose got up on its hind legs and came down hard on the hood with its hooves. Then it backed up a bit and came at the Land Rover, forgetting altogether about Uncle Rick inside.

Uncle Rick gave the horn a good workout.

The moose kept charging and jumping on the hood. Then he got a lucky strike. He moved the Land Rover about a foot towards the edge of the road, where the next stop was 500 feet below.

The moose charged and jumped on the hood for a few more minutes, and by then Uncle Rick's Land Rover was in a sorry state.

He tried to rev the engine one more time. That was enough for the moose. Somehow it managed to kick a hole in the radiator. The engine conked out.

Uncle Rick opened the door, and got ready to run for it. Early on, the moose had decided against any foot passengers along the road to Malkow Lookout. It came up on the driver's side and pushed. The Land Rover was screeching and groaning, rocking back and forth.

Uncle Rick was pretty sure the moose wasn't going to leave gracefully. Sure as hell, Uncle Rick wasn't going to leave gracefully either. He didn't want to get a quick trip back down the mountain and miss his visit with Trapper Art. Dad said he guessed not. They had a lot to talk about, them dating twins and all. Mom said, "A.E., for Christ's sake, let Rick finish his story!"

Uncle Rick had come up with an idea. Just before the moose decided what to do next, Rick rolled the window down a bit more, scooped some of Grandma's famous lemon meringue pie onto his left hand, and smeared it on the front windshield.

The moose stopped. He sniffed. He gave one more big push to the Land Rover, enough to send the back wheel up and over the edge of the bend in the road. That 500-foot drop was inching closer. When Uncle Rick looked down, he noticed that the trees were spaced just a foot wider than a Land Rover. He thought it would be hard to open the door if he made it. And he knew if he went over it wasn't likely he'd be worrying about opening the door to get out of his Land Rover.

The moose had a taste of Grandma Mulvaney's lemon meringue pie. As soon as the moose finished his treat, Uncle Rick repeated the exercise. Except in different order. The moose licked first, then kicked at the Land Rover. Uncle Rick scooped out more pie.

Moose don't move too fast, and they seem to have trouble making friends. By Uncle Rick's reckoning, he'd only know the moose about fifteen minutes.

Things weren't going that well, and it didn't look like they were going to be pals.

Uncle Rick was about to give up hope of ever getting to the top of Malkow Lookout to see his pal Trapper Art when he heard a loud noise. There was Trapper Art, banging together the tops of two garbage cans. Real slow. And real loud. Uncle Rick says they sounded like a drummer at a funeral, and he hoped like hell the funeral wasn't going to be his.

"Hi, Rick," says Trapper Art. "Did you get my Coca-Cola? I could use one about now."

Uncle Rick told Trapper Art that he was kind of busy.

"So I see," says Trapper Art.

"What took you so long?" says Uncle Rick.

"Oh, I heard you on the first honk. I've been up on that ledge there, watching you."

Uncle Rick says that he called Trapper Art a couple of names that we kids can't hear. I said there's only me here Uncle Rick, and I promise I won't tell the other kids. Heck, I said, I hear a lot of names and words from these two. Mom and Dad glared at me, so I decided I would just let it be and never learn what kind of names Uncle Rick called Trapper Art.

"Anyway," says Uncle Rick.

By then the moose was tired of all the talk. It leaned on the side of the Land Rover, pushing it closer towards the edge of the road, the side crumpling against a rock. Which, said Trapper Art, was the only thing holding Uncle Rick at the top of the road to Malkow Lookout.

Uncle Rick was getting as tired of the activity as the moose. He decided to check just how close he was to the edge. He opened the right door and looked out. And straight down. To somewhere he didn't want to go. That's when he decided to exit his vehicle. He hopped in the back of the Land Rover and rolled down the left window. He grabbed a couple of Cokes, and stuffed them in his back pockets.

He grabbed what remained of the pie and another Coke. Then he opened the back door.

Trapper Art was so interested in what Uncle Rick was doing that he forgot to bang the lids. "Art!" says Uncle Rick. "Bang. Bang."

Besides not making friends, moose don't have good memories. It turned around to see what the noise was all about. Uncle Rick had the pleasure of the moose's arse end in his face, and he used his extra bottle of Coke to best advantage. He took the bottle and whacked the moose on the butt three times. The moose figured out his arse-end was hurting when Uncle Rick hauled off and hit the moose once more for good luck, "Right where it hurts." That moose let out a wail like nothing he or Trapper Art had ever heard.

It jumped about ten feet forward, almost on top of Trapper Art.

Good thing Art's used to hopping away from things like traps, says Uncle Rick. He made it up to the ledge to his favorite seat in about four steps.

The moose didn't have a beef with Trapper Art. He was more interested in the Land Rover that tasted like a lemon meringue pie.

While this was happening, Uncle Rick grabbed a bag with a loaf of bread, some fresh ham, a few tomatoes and five pounds of sugar.

He still had a hold on Grandma Mulvaney's lemon meringue pie.

Uncle Rick took a flying leap out the back, just about the same time the moose hit the front. It took only one more wallop to dislodge the rock. And Uncle Rick's Land Rover.

During his way up the bank and the Land Rover's end-over-end roll down, Uncle Rick lost his balance for a second. Just enough to lose his grip on the pie. It turned in mid air, then landed bottom down. Right in front of the moose.

While Uncle Rick and Trapper Art drank their Cokes, the moose became a fan of the pie that made the Telkwa Café famous.

Trapper Art radioed the Telkwa Ranger Station and Ben Rollings came part-way up the road to pick up Uncle Rick. He stopped the Forest Service truck a few hundred yards down the hill, at a bit of a turn-around, and honked the horn just in case the moose was still around.

Though Ben looked for it, the Land Rover was hidden in the bush and rocks below, so all he could do was march up past Grandma Mulvaney's empty pie plate and holler for Uncle Rick.

Hilda put up a big stink because she had liked the Land Rover for its safety. She said she wasn't sure any more, and thought they should get a nice Chevrolet or Ford car.

Uncle Rick reminded her that the only thing that saved him was the Land Rover, until the moose sent it flying. He told Hilda that there was another vehicle just like it in Vancouver. If she worked things right, he could borrow a truck for the winter and in the spring, they could take the train to Vancouver for their honeymoon, and drive back home in their new Land Rover.

Hilda is now telling everyone that she's going to suggest to Uncle Rick that they pick a nicer color than the beige that was on the last one.

No one has the heart to tell her that they pretty well only come in that color. Nana says Hilda will have lots of surprises on her honeymoon, so one more won't make that much difference.

All That Glitters

Tuesday, October 4, 1960
Dear Maggie:

Thanks for the nice card and scarf for my birthday.

I'm not sure if you heard the news about the big accident at the corner two weeks ago. Right in the middle of town!

I swear that not one truck or car passed Mrs. King's, where Grandma Mulvaney, Patty Phelps and I were playing bridge. It was an exceptionally warm day, and we were on the screened porch. Mr. King was over at the Telkwa Barbecue grounds, fixing a few of the rocks in the barbecue pit. Outside of us ladies bidding, we were quiet, too.

After the game, I decided to leave and not stay for cake. I had work to do for the Women's Institute Meeting the next day. There was a lot of preparation because of the Thanksgiving Tea, and the fund raising for the Stoddards.

Even though the road isn't busy, I like to look both ways just to be sure. I stepped away from the front gate. It's hard to see because of Mrs. King's rose arbour, so I took another step towards the road.

As I did, a red car zoomed past me. It was going a fair clip. Until the corner caught it.

The car went right into the big log that is used to mark the corner. It picked up the log and dropped it right in front of the car window, on the lap of the driver. Glass and stuff flew everywhere.

The Kings are only about fifty feet from the corner, and Doc MacPherson is right next door, so I ran over there. Luckily, he was just having a break at home.

We both stopped when we walked onto the side of the road. I thought there was water all over the ground. We got closer and the water took shape and color. It was a few seconds before I figured out what was on the ground. For as far as we could see, there were jewels, sparkling in the sun.

Doc MacPherson and I ran to the driver's door. The man inside was sitting straight up, and he had a piece of glass sticking out the corner of his right eye. It must have gone in deep, because there was no blood.

The steering wheel and the log were pressing in the man's lap.

Jewellery was all over the road, yet strangely not in the car.

Mrs. King phoned Constable Reems in Smithers, and he called the ambulance. He told her that it would be about half an hour before it could get there, because the attendants were on their way back to town with a pregnant woman and they'd have to drop her at the hospital before they drove the twelve miles to Telkwa.

We tried to do what we could for the man. Doc MacPherson asked him if he could move his arms, feel his feet or move his toes.

The man turned his head towards me and looked right at me. He was trying to blink, but the glass got in the way. Doc MacPherson asked me to hold the man's hand. I reached in the car, and his hand was very warm. It surprised me, because I was expecting him to be cold and clammy, due to shock.

Doc MacPherson put his left hand on the man's forehead and with his right hand slowly and steadily drew the piece of glass out of the man's eye. He stayed absolutely still. I never felt any pressure on my hand, so can only guess that he was in such a state of shock that he never felt a thing.

Next, the man talked to us as if nothing had happened. He told us he was a jewellery salesman, on his way to Prince Rupert.

He didn't see the corner because he was eating a sandwich and a piece fell on his tie. He was trying to clean it because he only had the one tie.

Mrs. King had called the Telkwa Fire Department and in the next twenty minutes, seven firemen showed up. They tried to lift the log off the man, but it was wedged too tight, and Doc MacPherson was worried about hurting him with the sudden movement. Jack Rose suggested that they could cut away part of the log, and the firemen could hold what was left, then slowly lift it off the poor fellow.

The ambulance arrived about half an hour later, and by then the logging operation had begun.

Doc MacPherson kept checking his heart and he said it was ticking— strong and true. He gave the man a painkiller—something to stabilize him, but not knock him out. They needed him to remain conscious. That's where we came in.

For nearly three hours, your Grandma Mulvaney, Patty Phelps, Mrs. King and I took turns leaning into the car, holding the man's hand and talking to him.

His name is Wilfred Evans, and he's from Vancouver. He has a wife and four children. He even supplies Fern's Specialty Shop in Terrace. Your Mom has bought costume jewellery at Fern's, and it would be from Wilfred Evans.

It was strange. Mr. Evans was calm. He stayed awake. He said he didn't mind being there, because we were with him. He said he could feel our prayers washing over him. It was very peaceful and quiet.

Even more strange is that outside of us and the firemen and ambulance drivers and Doc MacPherson, no other cars came by the road all the time we were there. In fact, no one seemed to be around but us. It was like God had put a glittery shield around us, and no one but those who could help Mr. Wilfred Evans was allowed inside.

The firemen were sweating as they held the log as steady as they could. Mr. Evans only groaned once, and that was when the end of the log fell away after Jack Rose cut through it with his power saw.

When the firemen released the log and picked the steering wheel off Mr. Evans' lap, we all held our breaths. Everyone moved back as Doc MacPherson bent down to look at Mr. Evans' legs. He got up pretty fast, and asked me to go hold Mr. Evans' hand again. By that time, the firemen had brought a few chairs from Mrs. King's porch, so it was a sight, I am sure. Four ladies sitting on their bridge chairs, while our bridge table held medical equipment and a pile of costume jewellery. It seemed like a lifetime ago that we were sitting on the chairs at the bridge game.

Doc MacPherson told the ambulance driver that Mr. Evans one leg was so badly crushed that it would be very hard to lift him out without the leg being braced. It took another 45 minutes to brace the leg. I just stayed there, holding his hand. The other ladies busied themselves by running back and forth between Doc MacPherson's house and the car. Mrs. King kept going inside her house to get more bedding. By the time Mr. Evans was ready to be moved onto the stretcher, half of the King's belongings were out on the road.

When they moved him, Mr. Evans just looked at me and smiled. He said, "Thank you."

Once he was in the ambulance, it took a few more minutes to ready him for the ride to the hospital.

Doc MacPherson quickly took me aside and said he was sure Mr. Evans would never walk again. And, he might not make it.

I said, "He will make it. He has faith and he has our prayers. It's a sure thing. Mr. Evans will live."

The ambulance doors were shutting when I saw Doc MacPherson leaning over Mr. Evans, and reaching for his hand.

The glittery shield wore off as they drove away. Cars and people on foot began to arrive.

What a day. Grandad came down and helped direct traffic. The firemen helped pick up Mr. Evans's jewellery. Once the word spread, it was busier on the road than during the Telkwa Barbecue.

Everyone came to see the accident and once they heard what happened, they prayed for Mr. Wilfred Evans.

Early the next morning, Doc MacPherson came to the door. He told us that he'd had to amputate both of Wilfred Evans' legs at the Smithers Hospital.

And he told us that Wilfred Evans would live.

We went to see him in the Smithers Hospital. The Telkwa Volunteer Fire Department and Kinsmen paid for his wife and their oldest son to travel from Vancouver on the bus. We've given them your Mom and Auntie Polly's old rooms to stay in while they're here. The firemen are taking turns driving them in to Smithers.

All that time in the car, and Mr. Evans never complained about the pain. He kept thanking us for our kindness. I hope you will pray for him, Maggie. He has a long, long road ahead of him. Ironic, because he is a travelling salesman.

Love Nana

P.S. Tell your Mother.

Thursday, October 13, 1960
Dear Nana:

We had heard about Mr. Wilfred Evans, because he is now in the Terrace Hospital. They are waiting for him to get a bit better before the Kinsmen pay to fly him back to Vancouver. Dad went to see him. Jack Rose asked Dad to pay a visit because Dad used to be a Telkwa fireman, and he is a Kinsmen. Mrs. Evans and their son had to go back home, so Mr. Evans is all alone. Dad says it is remarkable how well he is doing and what a good mood he is always in. Yes, Nana, I agree. If you pray for people who are hurt, they will get better. We prayed for Mr. Evans.

Today, Ronnie and I got our hair cut. We think it is time to act a bit older, so my hair went from past my waist to just below my shoulders. Hilda wasn't too thrilled when I told her I wanted to look older, and closer to her and Martha's age. My hair is still so 'Toni' wavy—thanks to Trapper Art—that it took a lot of work to convince the hairs to do what I wanted. Ronnie only got a split ends trim, because she says she knows what's best for her hair, and is growing it past her rear-end. I should have just gone for a trim, too, because by the time I'd waited for Ronnie, my hair was waving all over again.

Martha is down visiting Hilda, and she's working in the shop. It is interesting to see them together, being identical twins and all. Except for the hair color, they do look alike. Those two are cooking something up, and it has to do with Uncle Rick and Trapper Art. Martha did Ronnie's hair for free. Hilda told me that because I am family, I will never have to pay to get my hair cut again. All the women in our family are such good customers anyway, says Martha. She says she almost feels like family, too. As I think of Trapper Art as mine, that Martha Throckmorton better not be thinking about Trapper Art as hers. Mom says I have to send the twins a thank you note, because they are so nice to Ronnie and me. I am not sending a thank you note to Martha. Hilda—OK. Ronnie sent the note to Martha and signed my name for me. Then she put a P.S. on the bottom and told her I was busy writing a letter to Trapper Art, and that's why she had to sign my name. I should hit her for that one. But I won't!

I am putting the note for Martha in your letter, because she is heading home tomorrow, and I don't have her box number in Telkwa. When you go to get your hair done next, would you please give her the card? Thanks, Nana!

Martha told everyone at the shop that I'm your granddaughter. Then we heard all over again about you and the Jehovah, and stringing the lights to Hell. It sure made the ladies laugh. Ronnie's Mom was there and she hadn't heard that one before. Then Martha started in on the Smithers Skating Club Ice Follies, and I wanted to crawl out from under Hilda's Heavenly Hair dryer and run for the hills, or home, which ever I hit first! I stuck it out, because after all, I was at the Ice Follies, and Martha asked me for a demonstration of Eileen Dover's skating ability, especially the splits. Because I'm such a good dancer, says Martha. She also let me say a couple of the punch lines.

It is pretty funny. Still embarrassing. I blame you for that, Nana. It is sometimes not that easy being your granddaughter, even from 150 miles away!

Patsy from Northern Drugs was at the shop and I thought she was going to blow a fuse. Hilda had to run to get her a Kleenex and a glass of water. Ronnie's Mom had to take off her glasses, and she couldn't stop shaking. She was trying not to laugh because of Ronnie and me. Once we walked outside, Ronnie's Mom fell over on the Southam's car, and then flopped against Hilda's Heavenly Hair Salon's wall. We thought something had happened to her. She was still laughing. She said to tell you that you are such a card. Yes. What a smarty-pants you are, Nana!

Love, Maggie

Saturday, October 15, 1960
Dear Maggie:

That was very nice of you to send a thank you letter to Martha. She hardly deserves all that praise, now that I hear she is telling stories about the Jehovah and me. Even though she was at the Women's Institute meeting when I gave the Jehovah his electricity lesson, she is just repeating a story of mine.

I don't think she should be letting you give demonstrations of Eileen Dover's skating show. That is taking it a bit too far. I might have to talk to her next time I'm in the shop. I saw her by Phelps & Saunders yesterday, and Hilda did a great job getting her hair toned down. It's a darker orange, and almost looks natural. This color goes well with her complexion. Seems like Trapper Art likes her any way she wears her hair.

We've been busy doing the fall yard work. Lots of things still are coming in from the garden. Grandad turned over the potato patch and got a hundred or so more spuds for the cold shed. Vern Hopkins delivered a chord of wood yesterday. Martin and two other Boy Scouts will be by to stack it in the woodshed later this afternoon. The coal comes in next week. Tell your Mother that I'm saving a bucket for her to use at New Year's.

Lots of Canada geese flying overhead. Feels like it might be a long winter.

Even though we fattened him up and let him go a few weeks ago, I hope Mr. Owl does OK this year. He sure as hell hasn't been back this way. The rabbits are getting thicker coats and Chico and Spotty are staying closer to the fire these days.

We're all excited about the Thanksgiving Tea next week. I wish you could be here, but I know that it is too much to come up for just an afternoon.

That damn Jehovah has been here again. He just won't give up. I think I'm going to have to go down to the Post Office one day soon.

Love Nana

P.S. Tell your Mother. I hear that Trapper Art and Martha are getting engaged. I hear that they are thinking of a spring wedding. A double wedding, with Uncle Rick and Hilda.

Oh, for Cripes sake. I don't believe it. MARTHA THROCKMORTON?????

Well, Dear

Nana did more than go down to the Post Office.

It was Saturday, October 22nd , about 4:30 p.m. I was home alone when she called, thinking about the fun they'd be having at the Thanksgiving Tea.

When I answer the phone, Nana says, "Just a moment, Maggie, dear."

I swear I hear tea being poured.

"Yes, two lumps, thanks," says Nana. "Oh, a biscuit. How nice of you, dear!"

I holler like hell into the phone for Nana to cut the B.S. with whoever is pouring the tea and tell her to talk to me. Turns out it is Constable Reems himself. He asks to speak to me. Nana just hands the phone over without another word.

Constable Reems asks to speak to Mom. "She's not here." Then he asks me if she is at work, and what's her number.

"She doesn't work. She's down at the Super Value picking up some Noxzema for Nana because it's on sale."

"Well, Maggie," he says. "What's your Dad doing right now?"

I tell him that Dad is away prospecting with Uncle Rick and Trapper Art.

"Where?"

"Up Hudson's Bay Mountain." That's near Smithers, I add, just to show him I wasn't falling for any tricks from him.

I ask if I can speak to Nana.

He says, "Not right now, dear." I HATE it when they call me dear!

104

"Well," I say. Nana can get away with a 'well' that brings the house down, so I thought that was a good start. Then I keep quiet.

"Hello?"

"I'm still here," I say.

"Oh, Maggie, dear, I really have to talk to your Mom or Dad."

I tell him that if they aren't around, I am the next closest living relative to Nana so he better put her back on the phone.

Next thing, I'm talking to Nana. She's still being so sweet; I know she's in real trouble.

"What the hell is going on, Nana?"

"Now, dear, don't you use profanity around your grandmother."

"WHAT? Nana! It's Maggie you're talking to!" I get worried then and there. My Nana is in deeper shit than my Dad and his cesspool.

Then I think to ask why she is having tea with Constable Reems in the first place, and why he is pouring it for her.

"Well, dear. I'm here in Smithers, at the RCMP Station."

She is selling me her Irish charm and I don't buy it. Not one little nickel's worth.

"What happened?"

"Well, dear," she says, "Remember that nice young fellow, Mr. Lennard? He's the one who delivers those pamphlets to your Grandad and me each week."

"Nana! Cut the crap. It's me, Maggie. What did you do and who is Mr. Lennard?"

"Well, dear. He's the Jehovah fellow. You know."

"Jesus Christ, Nana! What did you do?"

"Now, Maggie. That is enough of your profanity. I am sure Constable Reems can hear you bellering over the telephone. Well, dear, it started ... oh; just wait a minute, Maggie."

I hear Grandad's voice come close to the phone.

He says, "What, handcuffs?"

Nana mumbles something and it is obvious she has covered the mouthpiece. Nana comes back on in a few seconds, and says, "Well, dear. Grandad, Auntie Polly and Uncle Dan are here. I have to go talk to Constable Reems now. Will you be a good girl and tell your Mother to call me in care of the Smithers RCMP? Bye bye, dear. I love you!"

Click.

Oh, my. Nana is in deep, deep SHIT. She never even gave me hell when I said J.C. and even I know I can't get away with swearing like that, with Nana, or anyone!

I take off out of the house and hop on my bike. I roar along our driveway, out onto the main road, and peddle as fast as I can towards town. It usually takes me ten minutes, but I am going so fast I cut my time by three minutes.

I am at the corner of Lakelse Avenue, and stoplight number 1 is just turning orange. I see Mom and our car coming along. She is to my right, and I have gathered enough speed that I lean into the corner before the light turns red.

I'm usually a careful bike rider. Something makes me look away, just as I take the corner. Whap. I run right into the only parked car in the entire town of Terrace. It is Fern's car, and for some reason she has parked it a block away from her shop. The car is facing the wrong way, yet Fern has done a perfect park job.

I go head first onto the hood and grab hold of the windshield wiper, which stops my fall onto the pavement. Kind of.

I am able to crawl off my half of the hood— just in time to flag Mom down.

She hollers out the window, "Maggie! Your blouse is undone! Where are your shoes?"

Crap! I've popped all the buttons off my blouse when I hit Fern's car. Good thing I am wearing a new bra from her shop. When I headed onto the hood, my shoes must have decided they weren't up for the landing, or they didn't want to go for the ride.

I begin shaking and crying.

Mom thinks I am upset about my bike accident. I tell her I'm fine, but that my hand and arm hurt, and I think I need to get a new right knee because I think I bust this one.

I half stagger, half limp, towards the car. Mom tells me to get in and says she'll patch me up at home.

Then she thinks to ask what was I doing, running into Fern's car?

I'd look at my knee by this time, and at the blood pouring from a three-inch long cut on the right side of my kneecap. As Mom turns the car around the corner, I check in the glove compartment for a Band-Aid. There is only a little baby one, about an inch long. It doesn't stick too well, and when I bend my leg back after sticking the Band-Aid on, it pops off one side. I try to push it back on my knee, but there is too much blood, and the poor little thing falls off onto the floor of the car.

Mom glares at me and asks again what I am doing downtown.

"It's Nana!" I sniffle.

"What?" says Mom.

"Your Mother. Nana," I say.

"Nana?"

"She's killed the Jehovah!"

Now it's Mom's turn to start shaking and crying. "Jee-Zuz H. Kee-Rist! I knew it was going to come to this. What happened?" Just for effect, Mom rolls her eyes about twenty times in one second.

People ask me where I get it from, the cursing and eye rolling. I tell Mom just how much I don't know about what happened to Nana.

Mom pulls the car over at this point. She shakes her head a couple of times, lets out a huge sigh and shuffles around in her purse, then her wallet. Out comes a crumpled piece of paper. It's in Mom's handwriting, and I distinctly see Constable Reems' name and number on it. I decide it is better if I don't ask how she already has his number.

Mom must be upset, because she's calmed down pretty fast and doesn't even looked at me to see if I'm bleeding on the car. And she doesn't ask me how I am.

We sit there for a couple of minutes, doing nothing.

Mom says, "Well, dear, I'll just take you to the Doctor's and then we'll go home and call Nana."

I tell her I'm fine, and to take me home and call Constable Reems.

We keep quiet on the way back home. It's only about a four-minute drive, anyway. I remember that my bike is lying at the corner of Lakelse Avenue, cuddled up to Terrace's only parked car. I mean to call Fern to tell her I've hit her car, but I forget as soon as I try to walk. I have to drag my one leg along the driveway. (My bike sits there for three days before I remember again, and Uncle Rick picks it up. He tells Fern that I owe her a new windshield wiper. And maybe a new hood.) But to be fair, she owes me a new knee. What with all I've been through buying bras from Fern, she and I can pretty well call it even.

Mom tries to call Nana and Grandad's a couple of times. Then she takes a stab at Auntie Polly's number. I tell her that they are with Nana and Constable Reems at the RCMP Station in Smithers. Mom finally hears me and calls the RCMP.

It takes forever for Constable Reems to come to the phone.

"It's Fran." She doesn't say anything else for over five minutes. My Mom just gets more and more pale. She spends most of the five minutes shaking her head back and forth, back and forth. She nods a bit, and rolls her eyes, too.

But she doesn't say one word.

Now I've known my Mom for years. It just isn't like her, not to keep up her end of any conversation, even with a Royal Canadian Mounted Policeman. I know things are getting worse. Mom's head is shaking faster, and she's looking more nervous than my cousin Verna did when Mom played her wedding march in polka time. Too bad we didn't have any Telkwa Hall Rum Punch about now.

She suddenly says "thank you" and hangs up.

She doesn't even look at me. Instead she walks right over to the cupboard where Dad keeps his Canadian Club, unscrews the lid, and knocks down a good, long swig. Mom doesn't even like rye.

She slumps onto a chair at the kitchen table.

My turn. "Mom! What did he say?"

"Well, dear."

"Jee-zuz-H. Kee-rist! I can't believe it! Two hours since I spoke to Nana and all anyone can say is, 'well dear'?"

"Maggie. That is quite enough. Don't swear. Especially don't even try to explain why you are using profanities and the Lord's name like that. It is not becoming."

Ha! Mom is coming around. She tells me that Constable Reems has suggested she come to Smithers, and to get there as fast as she can.

We pack a few things and are heading out the door. When Tippy tries to jump in the car with us, we remember to phone Uncle Rob and ask him to pick the dog up and keep her with them for a while. Mom makes me call, and tells me to act like nothing is happening. I don't have the heart to tell Mom that Uncle Rob has already heard Telkwa's side of the story from five different people, and he wondered when we were going to find out. He wishes us luck. I tell him that we need more than luck. We need everyone to pray for Nana Noonan. I don't get a chance to say goodbye, because he is screeching with laughter, and Mom is hollering at me to get in the car.

Mom drives the three hours to Smithers in about three-and-a-half. She is going slower than a fully loaded logging truck trying to make it up the Airport Hill outside of Terrace.

We stop at Uncle Rick's loaner Ford truck, which is parked along Highway 16 near the entrance trail to Hudson's Bay Mountain Glacier. Mom leaves a note for Dad, asking him to call us as soon as he gets near a phone. Not at home. At Nana's. She doesn't bother to explain. I can understand why.

I've never been in an RCMP Station. Mainly, I try to keep out of trouble. One criminal in the family is enough.

I have to pee so bad when we arrive that by the time I am finished, Mom is already sitting in Constable Reems' office. The door is closed, and two other RCMP's are sitting at their desks. I am chicken to make a run for Constable Reems' door, because the two Mounties are the same ones I've seen picking people up after fights at the Telkwa Hotel. They have darn quick reflexes, and I don't want to get mixed up with them. I might end up in a jail cell, and that would be too much for Mom to take, unless I got in with Nana. I doubt that would happen.

I try walking back and forth to get Constable Reems' attention. He doesn't even glance my way. I HATE being a teenager. No one thinks you understand a thing, or could help out in a time like this.

About half an hour goes by. The two Mounties leave their desks. It looks like Mom isn't budging, and Constable Reems sure isn't looking at me. He's writing. Looks like he has enough for a book, with all the paper he's used.

I decide to take a walk. A door is open at the end of the hall. I see Nana's foot. Taking a chance that she is alone, I leap into the room.

"Well, dear!"

I nearly choke her with hugs.

Nana can beat around the bush like nobody's business. She says that the Thanksgiving Tea was a big success, and that they raised a lot of money for the Women's Institute and the Stoddards. I suggest that she is stalling, and if she'd like, she can just finish the story, like she did the Jehovah.

Nana doesn't even smile. She says nothing about my being funny, nor does she call me a 'card'—or, better yet—say that I'm 'just like her.'

The way her right foot is tapping and twitching, I know she is in a nervous mood. I don't see it often, but when I do, it is a sure sign that Nana has gone too far with something. And it usually means that Grandad or Mom get hauled in to deal with the townsfolk or our close family friend, Constable Reems of the Royal Canadian Mounted Police.

When she starts whispering, I'm not sure she's talking to me.

"Maggie. Lean over, and listen closely."

I don't have much choice, she is speaking so low. I move my legs sideways in the chair. I try not to think about my knee and really concentrate on what Nana has to say.

Nana tells me that Damn Jehovah was on his regular Saturday rounds and ended up in the alley behind the Anglican Church, just as the Thanksgiving Tea was breaking up.

The husbands were waiting in the alley. They had parked behind the church so they could have a smoke and not get caught by their wives, or Nana, who would normally tell them to smoke somewhere else, and not near God's house. The real reason is that she doesn't like cigarette butts sprinkled around the church parking lot or in 'her' alley.

There are a lot of things Nana doesn't like in 'her' alley. Number one is the Jehovah.

Nana tells me that she was the first to leave the church, because she invited the Women's Institute ladies to take the money to her place and count it on her large dining room table. The bonus was that Grandad is very good in math and he could double-check their adding.

"Nana! Please." I try one of her and Mom's tricks that usually works on me.

As Nana was telling the men off about their cigarette butts, along came Tyee Mary. Nana had saved some of her baking from the Tea for Mary and Old Joseph. No matter how many times Nana has invited her, Tyee Mary reminds her that Indians don't go to Teas.

There are a few of the women from church who remind Tyee Mary that Indians are not invited to teas, more like it. I just figured out the reason Nana brings out her best china teacups and cuts the sandwiches and cakes into nice designs when Mary visits. It's hard to be an Indian in Telkwa. But it is better than other places. Of course, it is hard to be Nana's granddaughter in Telkwa, too. I think it's going to get harder. Never as hard as it is for Tyee Mary, though. And she hasn't done anything to anybody.

"Nana, tell me what happened." I try to reason with her, and it works.

Tyee Mary was dropping off some smoked salmon in turn for a few jars of canned fruit and vegetables, and Nana's baking.

As they opened the gate and began walking towards Nana's house, the Jehovah came out of the porch. Nana says it may have been because she had the audience of all the husbands, or because Tyee Mary was right beside her, that she might have spoken a bit louder than usual.

Nana suggested that the Jehovah move his arse off her property and head towards Hell.

The Jehovah stopped. After all the years she'd known him not to look her in the eye, this time he stared right at her with his buggy, watery blues.

In a low voice—so only Nana and Tyee Mary could hear—he said, "Hello, Indian lover. I have to help you today or you will be in this state forever."

Nana was so shocked, she walked right past the Damn Jehovah and tore open the screen door. She pushed the kitchen door open and hopped inside so fast, the husbands had to lean way over the fence to see where she went.

Tyee Mary knew better than to follow Nana. She wandered over with her rucksack full of fish and sat down on a bench near the barn.

The first thing that came out of the house was Nana's trusty 410 shotgun. She followed right after, and loaded the gun with fresh buckshot right in front of the Jehovah, the husbands—who had entered the yard by now—and Tyee Mary, who jumped up when she saw the gun.

That poor Jehovah was pretty well stuck to the ground. It was just like he'd smeared the same goop that he uses to hold his hair in place on the bottom of his shoes. The hairs that are left, added Nana.

She can be a pretty good storyteller when she gets going.

Nana said that she must have lost her head for a moment. At the top of her lungs, she bellered, "Move your bigoted arse-end off my property."

"NOW!"

That did it for the Jehovah. His feet miraculously became unstuck and he must have risen a foot in the air. As he was facing the porch, he mistakenly took shelter there.

Nana was on his tail. As she had the 410 advantage, the Jehovah realized that his escape route now had become a dead end.

Nana had never heard him talk in more than a few words, let alone scream. She wanted to stop him, but didn't. She almost laughed about the postcard from Hell, then thought better of it.

She was so mad, she couldn't think of what to do next. So she stayed quiet for a second or two.

Then she told the Jehovah that maybe he was right after all.

"I've actually thought a lot about my salvation lately," said Nana, in her loudest, clearest voice.

That stopped everyone up. Especially the Jehovah.

Nana saw an opportunity. She hopped over the doorsill and tried to pull the screen door shut.

For once, that Damn Jehovah moved faster than Nana. He began pulling like hell on the screen door, with Nana tugging at the latch from inside. It was a moment or so before she realized that there was one damn Jehovah foot between her door and the screen.

She still had her shotgun in her left hand, because she is left handed.

Slowly, she levelled the shotgun between the space, the screen door and the Jehovah.

"Oh, Nana!"

I'm nearly falling off my chair. My eyes are bugging out and my heart is pounding. Probably a bit like the poor Jehovah's.

"Mom!"

"Maggie!"

In walks Mom and Constable Reems. The look on their faces makes me glad that Nana is there to protect me.

"Well, dear?" says Mom to me. I keep quiet and look over at Nana.

"Well, dear," says Nana. Then she sits back and crosses her arms. She's not going to say one more thing.

Constable Reems says, "Well—" then thinks better of adding the word 'dear' in this crowd.

Mom asks Nana what she did.

I had a little accident, she says.

Little, says my Mom.

Well, dear, little to me.

Mom says not so for the poor bloody Jehovah. "For Christ's sake, Mother!"

"Well, dear," says Nana.

That's it. I start giggling. One too many 'well dears' for me.

Both Mom and Nana glare at me. "Maggie. Stop it."

I say, "Well, dears, I can't!" I get so worked up that I'm squeaking and squirming and trying to laugh out loud, but all that happens is I get wheezy and sweaty. Constable Reems is sent to get me a Kleenex and a glass of water. He is looking at me kind of funny, and is red-faced. Then he frowns and stares at my front. (And my nice new bra from Fern's Specialty Shop.)

"Are you OK, Maggie?"

"Yeah. Why?"

"Well, dear. All the buttons on your blouse are open."

All of a sudden, Mom and Nana are surprised at my appearance. Nana reaches in her left shoulder area and comes up with a safety pin.

"Go fix yourself up, Maggie," says Mom.

I get sent to the car to do it. I regret that I've forgotten my sweaty Kleenex and glass of water. I realize that I didn't bring any clothes, only underwear and shoes. Four pairs, mind you. I decided to change my shoes to make the trip to the car worthwhile.

I know damn well that they are talking about important stuff back there, and I'm missing it!

Just as I finish wiping the blood from my very sore knee and hand with good old spit and the corner of my blouse, Mom and Nana march out of the RCMP Station and hop into the car.

Mom grabs the steering wheel and stares straight ahead. She's got a grip on the wheel like Johnny Williams did on the horse's reigns back at the Telkwa Barbecue Rodeo.

Nana gets in the back seat, behind Mom. She stares out the window, at what seems the most interesting view she's ever looked at.

I jump out of the front passenger seat, bound for the back seat. I want to be near my Nana Noonan.

"Get back in the car, Maggie. Now! Sit in the front seat," bellers Mom.

She scares me so much am in the front seat again before I get a chance to touch the back door handle. One growl from Mom, and I'm doing as I'm told.

While I am rearranging myself and my safety-pinned blouse, I have a real good look at Nana. She is fidgeting with her purse. She never does that. Boy, oh, boy. She is in some trouble.

"Where are we going now?" I say with as much enthusiasm as I would when we are doing something really exciting.

"We're going home."

"Home, to Terrace?"

"Yes."

"With Nana?" Things are looking up.

"No."

"Where's she going?"

Mom says she thinks Nana should be going to jail, but Constable Reems has taken a different approach.

I can't see Nana too well because it is dark out. I can hear her real well. When Mom mentions jail, Nana lets out a tiny gasp.

Now I'm really mixed up. "We're driving towards Telkwa, yet we're not staying at Nana's?"

"Nope. Uncle Dan is waiting at the edge of Telkwa, and we'll meet him there. Nana will go home with him."

I suggest that it will be easy for me to go home with Nana, because I can catch the train on Sunday afternoon, still have time to get my clothes ready for school, and get a good night's sleep for Monday.

"That is not necessary, Maggie. You are coming home with me."

I tell Mom that I know exactly what happened. Well, right up to the part when Nana shot the Jehovah. I remind Mom that we have to stick together, and she can't treat Nana like that, after all she's been through today. Anyway, she didn't mean to shoot the Damn Jehovah. And he was on her property.

Nana could be bound and gagged in the trunk, for all the noise not coming from the back seat.

Real quiet, Mom says, "His name is Calvin Lennard."

"Whose name is Calvin Lennard?"

"The Jehovah. His name is Calvin Lennard."

I tell Mom that I don't care. I am going to call him that Damn Jehovah until Hell freezes over, or Nana gets it wired for electricity. I say that a bit too bravely.

"Maggie. Please."

Poor Mom looks like she's about had it for the day. I catch a glimpse of her as we drive past the last streetlight on the way out of Smithers. I decide it might be better to push my luck when there's someone on my side.

"OK, Mom. Let's go home."

"Thank you, Maggie."

Oh, oh. Mom must not know what really happened, or she would be taking this differently. She would be at least a bit mad at the Jehovah, for what he said to Nana and Tyee Mary. And I'll bet she would still be mad as hell at Nana. At least she would have a reason.

Nana is sure keeping her lips pressed together. For the first time in history.

Mom is driving the twelve miles to Telkwa like we're going to a funeral. The lights are on in the car and she's topping about 5 miles per hour. It's night-time, we'll give her that, but cows in the field could walk faster than this.

At this speed, there is nothing to do but drift off to sleep. My knee is so sore I squirm around trying to get comfortable. No use. This is going to be a long night, no matter who you are.

Mom jerks the wheel to the right, guns the car and flicks the lights onto bright. Our car and us bounce over something and we propel along a road I don't even know exists. Tree branches hit the car, surprised as hell to be woken up. To show that they are none too pleased, they decide to leave a nice gouge in the driver's door. They won't put up with stuff like that.

We stop. Fast. The dust rolls in and around us, just like it did on Johnny Williams when dove off Destiny the horse, his makeshift diving board. I am trying to think of funnier times. It isn't working.

She's shut off the lights.

Mom says, "Get out of the car."

I obey, and open the door. Then I get the "Maggie. Please."

I get it. Mom meant Nana.

"Where is she going to go here in the middle of nowhere and in the dark?" Cripes. Nana should have stayed at the RCMP Station. At least they gave her some tea and biscuits. Her own daughter! Remind me never to get in shit with my Mom. I am beginning to think an Irish temper runs in the family. I must have gotten the Mulvaney temper, because we just get mad and get over it. Mostly.

Out of the corner of my right eye, I see something glowing. It's a cigarette. The way the thing is glowing, I know it's Uncle Dan. The way he sucks on the thing, and the lighted end goes up about an inch, I know he is none too happy, either.

Mom turns the lights on again. Uncle Dan must not have expected that, because he jumps a good two feet towards us, and lets out a half-yipe, half-swear word that I am not allowed to repeat.

"Holy shit, Fran! What did you do that for?"

"What'd I do what for?"

"Turn the lights on like that."

"I don't know. But it was fun to see you jump." Mom starts laughing. Not her regular ha-ha-ha, either. Uncle Dan starts snorting and laughing right along with Mom. I take the opportunity to open the car door.

"Maggie! Shut the damn door. Stay in the car."

I take my merry time doing as I am told and manage a real long glance at Nana. She is not laughing. She is looking straight ahead. Now, that's a new one on me. My suspicions are confirmed: Nana Noonan is in more trouble than I had even guessed. Even on her worst day, she would have fallen out of the car laughing to see her prized son-in-law jump like that.

I get a sinking feeling in my gut. Could be that we haven't eaten all day, but I am pretty sure that it is because I can now clearly see Ben Rollings behind Uncle Dan. Inside Wee Mary Rollings car. Oh. My. Mary does not let anyone drive her car, even Ben. If they have Mary's car, it is because they don't want anyone to know that inside the car is one Nana Noonan, being brought home and then being sent to her room. Maybe to stay forever!

Everything picks up speed. Nana jumps out of the car, comes around to my side and leans in the window. She hugs me, and gives me a quick peck on the cheek. She still smells of Noxzema, and faintly of the tea and biscuits she enjoyed at the RCMP Station in Smithers.

I start to say goodbye, and end up crying. I try to reach out for Nana but she is gone. I only have a chance to touch her cheek. My hand is wet from her tears.

Mom says, "Maggie. You've had enough for one day. Put your head down, and go to sleep."

I try to see what Nana is doing, as Mom backs the car around so fast that I slip forward and whack my already-buggered-up-forever kneecap on the glove compartment. No choice for me. I have to put my head down because I think I'm going to puke.

When I come to, Mom is opening my door, and telling me to get out, because we're home. The lights are on in the kitchen. Dad comes to the front door.

"Hey, you two!"

He'd left Uncle Rick and Trapper Art prospecting, because they decided to head up a creek bed that looked promising, and weren't going to come back for another week. As Dad had to be back to work on Monday, he'd walked out to the highway and hitched a ride with a forestry crew, coming back from a late-season forest fire.

I have to lie down. My knee is all swollen up; my hand hurting like hell and somehow I've lost the safety pin that held my blouse together.

I faintly hear my Dad ask Mom, "You want *another* rye?"

"What happened, Fran?"

"Well, dear."

Next thing I hear is Dad cursing away, none to quietly, "That old bat! She's done it now! Jee-zuz H. Kee-Rist!"

Do As Your Mother Says

October 29, 1960
Dear Maggie:

This might be the last letter I write for a while.

I want you to keep this in case you are asked to be a witness of my character. This is exactly what happened. It is the version I started to tell you at the RCMP Station in Smithers, only your Mother and Constable Reems broke up our private chat. I had to leave a few details out until now.

That damn Jehovah ended up in the alley behind the Anglican Church just as the Thanksgiving Tea was breaking up. The husbands were waiting for their wives. They had parked along the alley so they could have a smoke and not get caught. You know how I go on about them leaving their cigarette butts on the grounds of God's house and my alley. I had to take the opportunity when it was presented to me, so I lost a minute or so talking to the men.

I'm usually the last to leave the church, as Grandad and I always tidy up. Last Saturday, the ladies were coming across the alley to our place to count the money. I was the first to leave.

Just as I stepped into the alley from the Churchyard, Tyee Mary appeared. I'd asked her to drop by to pick up some extra baking from the Thanksgiving Tea, and the fruits and vegetables I'd canned for her, in exchange for jars of smoked salmon.

Well, out comes the Jehovah from my yard. I did have a bit of an audience, I'll admit. While the husbands were stomping madly on their smokes, I took the opportunity to strut just a tiny bit. (You know how I can get.) I told the Jehovah to move his arse towards Hell and not my place.

For some reason, that Damn Jehovah finally looked right at me, and in a low voice said, "Hello, Indian lover. I have to help you today, or you will be in this state forever."

Most of the men who were waiting for their wives are the ones we see in the park by the Post Office. What ever their religions, they had prayed for a moment like this. I have to credit Mr. Redfern. Auntie Polly told me that he had the foresight to nip inside the church hall to tell the wives that whoever bet on me today had better get outside, because the payout looked pretty big.

It didn't take long for quite a crowd to gather. One of the busy-bodies from the Catholic Church got on the phone and made one call. The spare half of town that didn't attend the Thanksgiving Tea and wasn't in the alley were likely on the Telkwa party-line phone, so pretty well everyone who cared to see the show received the notice.

No one spoke. They all waited, and were as still as Tyee Mary can be when she's down by the Post Office, trying to out-stand the Jehovah.

I stood as still as everyone else. The only thing that might have given me away was that my right eyebrow was raising all on its own, and it was damn near to my forehead. The Jehovah was shifting from foot to foot, eyeing me out of the corner of his buggy, watery blue eyes.

By keeping still for a moment, I had a chance to think about what that Damn Jehovah had said. That son of a bitch. Now everyone knew. He doesn't like Indians. And Tyee Mary was standing right beside me. I couldn't take that sitting or standing. She's my oldest friend, and she has a tough enough time of it. Indian or not, I won't put up with that crap. From anybody. And definitely not from the Jehovah.

I told him that on second thought, he might be right. I may need to be saved, or redeemed, or whatever it is that Jehovahs do to people. I told him I'd been thinking about salvation, and today was his lucky day. I said that as I was headed back into the house, he might as well come on down, bring his magazine, and we could have a chat.

By gosh, news travels fast in Telkwa. Trucks and cars were flocking in the alley behind the church. If only this many people turned up to Sunday service!

You know, I think that Jehovah thought he had me. He was strutting down our walkway. I just left the gate open, and nodded my head to the crowd. Half the town was in the yard by the time he and I made it to the porch.

Some of the Women's Institute ladies had arrived, so I asked them to go over by my garden seats, and sit with Tyee Mary. I told them that there was a bit of unfinished business for me to clear up with the Jehovah before we could go in to count the money from the Thanksgiving Tea.

I can see Constable Reems' point. There were a lot of people in the yard, and it could have been dangerous.

The Jehovah was standing just inside the porch, holding the screen door. I told him I was just going inside to get ready to meet my saviour.

I hopped over the doorsill, pushed the kitchen door open, and tried to pull the screen door shut. That Jehovah had a hell of a hold on the handle. He'd put his foot between the screen and the door to boot.

For some reason, he and I looked each other in the eye again. I didn't like what I saw. His look was like I see in people like Mrs. Rannerfan when she glares at Tyee Mary and thinks I'm not watching!

I don't give a good God Damn. If he were a Catholic, an Anglican or a Jehovah, he doesn't like Indians. I do. And I decided that it was time to show him what most of Telkwa is made of.

You know me. I'm still pretty quick with the reflexes. Damn quick. Too quick for him. Before he knew what happened, I'd reached around the back of the door and pulled out my trusty 410 shotgun. Right in front of him, I loaded it with fresh buckshot. Considering how mad I was, it is a good thing I only keep buckshot on the shelf above the kitchen door.

I levelled the gun at his foot, keeping in mind, he still had hold of the screen and his foot was displayed like a model's showing the latest in shoes, right in my own door-jam.

I said, very loud, so everyone could hear me, "Move your bigoted arse-end off my property. NOW!"

His eyes opened wider than usual. I swear the hairs plastered on his head moved back an inch.

He stood still for half a second. Then he hollered so bloody loud that the whole crowd jumped at one once.

"Mrs. Noonan, you will never be saved, and you are going to your Hell!"

I pride myself with practicing safety in handling firearms. The entire town expects that of me.

Maybe my reflexes weren't up to par last Saturday. Or he really startled me. My left hand whipped that gun out the space between the Jehovah's foot and the door stoop. Just as he jumped back. I think he realized he might have gone a bit too far.

The poor bugger. He was still holding on to the screen door handle. For dear life. He tried to turn and run for it, but by then the crowd was right at the back step.

I said, "Move it!" Pretty loud, if I do say so, because I had a sore throat for two days afterwards.

Guess that did it. That Damn Jehovah let the screen door fly shut, and it hit my hand. I had a good grip on the trigger, or so I thought. But the bloody gun went off, and the Jehovah dropped like the owl that was bothering our rabbits.

There was one big gasp from the crowd. It was the sound of them sucking their breath in at once.

No one moved.

Then I bent down and checked the Jehovah's pulse. He felt clammy, so I wasn't too worried. I ended up tending to him, just like the owl. Although I liked the owl better. With all his bellering and complaining, you would think that Damn Jehovah had been mortally wounded. I told him to shush up. Must have scared him, because I was reaching for the gun at the same time. He sure looked better when all I did was move the gun to the far end of the porch.

Grandad was in the house, and saw it from the kitchen window. Although he admitted to ducking once when the buckshot started flying. He's the one that called Constable Reems.

It didn't take long for the ambulance to arrive. Constable Reems was in the alley, talking to the crowd. He told Grandad that after writing down a few names, he realized that there were at least 350 people in the alley by the Anglican Church, and they were all dying to be witnesses. Constable Reems put his notebook back in his breast pocket and came in the yard to see me.

I had decided to sit with Tyee Mary in the garden. She was about the only person in town who didn't see the action. And here it was, partly in her honor.

Constable Reems told me not to go anywhere. He said he'd be back to see me right after he sent the last of the crowd home, and then right after he called the Smithers Hospital to check on the condition of the Jehovah.

Our good Constable Reems has been here a couple of times this past week. Things changed when the Jehovah's condition changed.

Now I have to stay in the house until this thing is settled. I dare not go out in the yard, other than to the outhouse. There is a regular congregation in the alley behind St. Stephen's Anglican Church. All day, right up to suppertime. Then they're back for an hour or two before bedtime. They all shout their approval when I stick my nose out the door. Good thing the weather is turning to heavier winter. The less hardy only spend an hour or two a day. I feel honoured that they are supporting me, but am not so sure about what will happen next.

Tyee Mary and Old Joseph came for a visit yesterday. They thanked me for sticking up for them. I said that they are doing the same for me, just by turning up. They both smiled and nodded, and gave me a beautiful blanket. Tyee Mary says it is to keep me warm in jail. We all had a good laugh over that. Even Grandad! He hasn't talked much to me this past week. He's been taking the dogs for long walks and he tries to read the paper from cover to cover. Then he gets up and takes the dogs for a walk again. Auntie Polly says he won't talk to anyone, not even her.

Constable Reems has gone to bat for me. He says I have to lay low for a few months. I might need a change of scenery, since it is going to be pretty hot over the winter here in Telkwa. I'm going to figure out what to do next week, when Constable Reems meets your Grandad, Mom, Auntie Polly and Aunt Sue and my 'solicitor' Jack Danford.

You are a good kid, Maggie. I am very proud of you. By seeing most of this first hand, I hope that you will have learned that there is a right way to do things and a wrong way to do things.

My heart was in the right place, but my temper got the best of me.

See you around. I hope!

Love Nana

P.S. Don't tell your Mother about this letter. She will have heard the story from Constable Reems by now. We don't want to bother her with all the details. That is, unless the Jehovah suddenly decides to presses charges!

Winter Break

Fran Mulvaney
Box 1365
Terrace, B.C.

Monday, November 7, 1960
Dear Mom:

Constable Reems says it's OK to come here. A.E. isn't so sure, but what can we do?

No one is going to press charges as long as this is the truth – when the Jehovah – I mean, when Mr. Lennard—came to your door and hollered like hell, he scared you.

Constable Reems says he believes you because your statement was the same as the poor Jehovah's. Now that's a good one. Your description of the buckshot ricocheting off the cement wall by the back door is the very same as his. The Jehovah admitted to holding on to the screen door and letting it fly. He says he might have spoken loudly to you. He says he didn't mean for the screen door to hit your gun hand. Most importantly, the fact that it was only his big toe you shot off is remarkably in your favor.

You made so many complaints about the Jehovah to the R.C.M.P. over the years, that for some reason, things are working for you.

My God, Mother! You managed to get enough witnesses.

There is one important thing for you to remember. Constable Reems says that you are absolutely forbidden to use, or even touch, your gun in Telkwa's town limits. If you ever pull it out again in town, Constable

Reems will have to fine you and you will be charged. There are to be NO exceptions. To be certain of this, he has told most every one of your "witnesses," which is nearly half the town, including the Jehovah. They are to keep an eye out and to let him know if your memory suddenly fades when a Jehovah walks by and you are overcome with nostalgia.

The R.C.M.P. Staff Sergeant has agreed that if you spend the winter with us in Terrace, by the time spring pops her head out of the snow, there will be a couple of new Jehovahs in Telkwa and all of you can go about your business.

Even though it was the Jehovah who was shot, he got in a bit of trouble with his church, for all the commotion you and he caused.

Don't think for one moment, Mother, that I hold the Jehovah—Mr. Lennard—to blame.

Just because all of Telkwa is treating you as some kind of heroine does NOT fly at our house. Polly, Sue and I are very disappointed in you. You stubborn old pain in the arse, Mother! We want you to get on with things and forget this ever happened.

Because it's you, we'll never be able to forget it. We'll just do what we can, and get on with things.

See you on Saturday.

Love from Fran

P.S. You are going to have to buck up on your target practice if you want to get into crime full time. Don't tell Maggie that the real reason you are coming here is to avoid jail time. No sense bothering her with all the details. Thank gosh the Jehovah isn't going to press charges.

What Goes Around, Comes Around

February 21, 1961
Dear Nana:

We sure miss you and Chico. It was so much fun having you here all winter!

I hope that you're enjoying things back home, and that Mom and Grandad managed to help you get all your geraniums back in their rightful spots on the window sills. Thanks for leaving me a couple. I promise to water them and pick off the dead leaves and blooms when they are finished.

Mom says we might have to get another dog, because Tippy is so lonely without Chico. Dad says as long as it is not another Chico, it would be O.K. with him.

I like it that we shared my room. And yes, you told me time and time again that I should never let my temper get the best of me. Don't worry. I think I got the Mulvaney temper, and not the Noonan one. Takes me a long time to get mad, and I always try to reason with my victim first. Oh! I mean I try to reason with whomever I'm not agreeing with. Ha ha.

By watching you back yourself into a corner of buckshot, I learned one very important lesson: Pick your fights.

I also learned to use humor more than temper, and the very most important lesson is that you should always leave your gun in the kitchen unless you are heading way out of town and have hunting on your mind.

Things are fine here. My team won their volleyball game at lunch hour yesterday. Mr. Kenney Powers has given us a book report to do for English and Social Studies. We have a choice of three subjects: the history of Terrace; the history of how our family came to the Terrace area (or the Northwest, in the case of some of the kids from other towns) or the history of either logging, fishing or mining in the Northwest.

I decided to write about you, and how your family came to Terrace. When we visit you in Telkwa at Easter, I'll have some questions for you. Maybe we could look through the shoebox of old photos to see what you have. I would only use those little triangle-shaped sticky black holders to keep the pictures in place.

Remember that Mrs. Simpson's dance class show is the weekend after Easter and you and Grandad promised to come down for it.

I miss you! See you at Easter.

Love, Maggie

February 21, 1961 7 p.m.
Dear Nana:

Don't tell Mom that I sent you this letter!

She said not to bother you, but I am sure you will want to know this.

Mrs. Dillard is renting rooms now that her family died and she has to make some money.

Ronnie and I only saw his back, but the man that moved in there today walks with a limp.

Love, Maggie

P.S. We're pretty sure it's the Jehovah.

The End ——————

Then What Happened?

Marking the Occasion of the 50th Anniversary of the Telkwa Women's Institute Fall Tea and Bake Sale

Saturday, October 7, 2000
By Maggie Mulvaney-Lawrence

Constable Reems was transferred from the Smithers detachment to Terrace after the set-to with Nana and the Jehovah. He moved on after a few years to RCMP Headquarters in Vancouver. Along the way, he met and married a woman named Nan. They had five kids. Constable Reems bought some land in Telkwa and retired there. He wrote a best-selling book about being a Royal Canadian Mounted Policeman, though he drove a car. He dedicated the book to Nana Noonan, who he says was his favorite citizen in any town, any where, in Canada. Now, that's quite an honor.

Auntie Polly and Uncle Dan Hale lived out their days in Telkwa. Their daughter Verna had three daughters with Ben before they divorced in the 1970's. She has remarried and lives in Vancouver. Outside of Nana, Martin is the only one to take formal electricity training. He is an electrical engineer. He married his high school sweetheart and they moved to Terrace. They have four grown kids, three boys and a girl. Martin and his wife are busy being grandparents.

Uncle Rob and Auntie Rene Mulvaney retired in Terrace. Uncle Rob passed away in the early 1980's at age 65. Robbie Jr. became a pilot and married a feisty young woman who already had two kids. Annie-Lee went on to become a nurse, and married a nice young fellow who was visiting the area from New Brunswick. They have one son and live in the sunny Okanagan. Auntie Rene is 75 and lives near Annie-Lee and her family in the Okanagan.

Aunt Sue Pike was 70 when she passed away from kidney failure in the early 1980's. Uncle Hank lives in their house along the road in

Hazelton. Willy Pike remained with the Royal Canadian Air Force until his retirement in the mid-1990's. He and his wife, son and daughter moved to Vancouver Island. Beth, Nan, and Jane Pike all married fellows from around the Pacific Northwest. Trudy met a fellow from back east and lives in the Ottawa area. The five Pike cousins have sixteen kids amongst them.

Uncle Rick Mulvaney and Trapper Art Lawrence married Hilda and Martha, the Throckmorton twins. Although they had a great party and everyone enjoyed themselves when they held a double wedding ceremony in the spring of 1961, all four of them agreed that they could never have matched the fun they had when cousin Verna got married at the Telkwa Hall. Rick and Hilda live in Terrace. They have twins. A boy, Art, and a girl, Edie. Trapper Art and Martha were married for a few years until she left him and Telkwa with a travelling salesman. She says he was away in the bush too much. She's right. He was. They had no children. And that is a damn good thing.

Auntie Meryl and Uncle Martin Sandburne sold the Telkwa Café after owning and operating it for twenty-five years. The townsfolk lost interest in the food once they left and the Café is now a youth drop-in center. Meryl and Martin had two daughters, Mandy and Lucy. They all moved to the Sunny South after they sold the café. Meryl and Martin missed the North, and now live near Mandy and her family in Prince George. Their oldest daughter Lucy lives in the sunny south, thank you very much.

Ronnie Southham became a hair stylist. She travelled the world for five years, and got lonesome for Terrace. When she moved back, she bought Hilda's Heavenly Hair Haven when Uncle Rick and Hilda had kids. Ronnie married a fellow from Nova Scotia and they have a girl and a boy. She does Hilda's hair now. We still see each other whenever we can.

Tyee Mary and Old Joseph lived their lives on the Reserve near Telkwa until their passing, one month apart, in 1999. They were both 99. Once in a while, especially in her last few years, Tyee Mary would ask one of her sons to drive her past the Post Office and the Royal Bank along Telkwa's main street. The car would slow down, then stop. Right in front of the Telkwa Hotel Bar. It didn't stay long. Just long enough for anyone watching to see Tyee Mary glance towards the spot where the Jehovah faithfully stood for all those years. She would throw her head back and laugh, as the car picked up speed and turned the corner to take Tyee Mary home.

Grandma Mulvaney never gave up making pies for her friends and family. She won more prizes for her lemon meringue pie at the Bulkley Valley Fall Fair than she could count. She lived a few more years in the Bulkley Valley Lodge Senior's Home in Smithers. With her family gathered at her side, Grandma Mulvaney was 84 when she died of a heart attack in 1981.

Fran and A.E. Mulvaney got tired of the weather in the North, so they did what many northerners do: in the 1970's, they moved to the Sunny South. Fran likes gardening and A.E. is still inventing things. They travel home to Telkwa and Terrace as often as they can. Not a day goes by when they don't comment on how their daughter Maggie is a lot like her Nana Noonan. They are thankful that Maggie never took up hunting.

What about me, Maggie Mulvaney? I lived in the North until I was in my late-twenties. After a few tries at romance, I gave up. Truth is, I never quite got over Trapper Art Lawrence. When I was in my early thirties, Trapper Art caught up to me again at the Telkwa Barbecue. We married soon after and now live with our dog and two kids in the sunny south. You will have guessed this: I'm a writer. Trapper Art got into doing television documentaries on the great outdoors. His show is syndicated in 120 countries worldwide. Our kids like to go to visit their Northern relatives. They always ask to hear the real scoop on Trapper Art and me, but never get too far because the stories always go back to Nana Noonan and the Jehovah. Oh, I mean Mr. Lennard.

Nana Noonan and Grandad lived in the house behind the Anglican Church in Telkwa for over sixty years. Grandad was 88 when he died of a heart attack. In 1984, when she was 90, Nana died of stubbornness and a bit from old age. Nana Noonan sure cared about people, especially her family. She made the acquaintance of a couple more tormentors over the years, but she never liked them half as much as she did that Damn Jehovah.

The Jehovah is now completely bald. He married Mrs. Dillard and still lives in Terrace. He walks with a very slight limp. In the early 1970's, with Mrs. Dillard's encouragement, the Jehovah got involved with Toastmasters. He really enjoys looking people straight in the eye when speaking to them. He can talk on any subject for at least three minutes, especially the Tall Totem Guest House, which he and Mrs. Dillard-Lennard own. He'd make Nana proud.

Relative History

Year-end Creative Writing Essay for Mr. Kenney Powers' Social Studies and English Class

By Maggie Mulvaney, Grade 8, Division B. Skeena Secondary School, Terrace, B.C.

My Nana, Annie Elizabeth Noonan, was one of four children born to an Irish mother and an Irish-Canadian father.

Great-grandfather's Canadian side of the family had ripped up their Irish roots in the mid-1800s.

They were proud to be Canadian. And they tried to forget where they came from. They spent the early years in their new country practising an upper Canadian Accent, and were not about to trade it, or their newly earned affluence and community importance, on a steamer trip back to a potato farm in Ireland.

The family did not see eye-to-eye with my great grandmother. She was too "Irish." Her children were just as bad, especially the girl, my Nana. The boys, Jimmy, Cecil and Tom, were incurably Irish. They played, laughed and tussled their way around their grandparent's house, yard and the fields beyond. They spent too much time enjoying life and it seemed that they had no cares in the world.

Their mother, my great-grandmother, spent a lot of time with them, encouraging them to enjoy being children first, before the hardships of life got in their way.

They didn't have to wait too long.

Nana's father was drowned in a well in a freak accident on the family's London, Ontario farm in 1903. Great-grandfather's family closed ranks

131

and said that they could not see, or give any money to their son's children because of their overwhelming grief.

Nana said great-grandfather's family, especially his Mother, treated them badly. She was jealous that great-grandfather was happy and in love with his wife and four young children. Great-grandfather was his mother's favorite, and she did not want to share him with anyone, particularly someone he loved.

I have heard, but haven't asked, that the Canadian side of the family were mad at my great-grandfather for travelling back to Ireland and going ahead and falling in love with great-grandmother when there was a perfectly good young Protestant woman in London, Ontario that would have done fine. There was plenty of bitterness, to be sure.

Great-grandmother was left near penniless, with four young children, ages 9, 7, 6 and 4. She had no one to turn to. Her family in Ireland wanted her to come back home. She should raise the family in a proper Irish Protestant household, they said.

The children were lively, well mannered and smart. They loved the open spaces of their Canadian home.

Great-grandmother had other ideas than to stick it out near her in-laws. She had a pioneer spirit. Maybe that was what made her look in the newspaper, one fateful day in the autumn of 1905.

Her and her children's lives changed forever when she answered an ad in the paper, and became a pen pal to a widower in Northern British Columbia. He had one son, Billy, and a dearly departed wife. He agreed that more children were fine as he surveyed the expanse of his large vegetable farm. We have some of their letters. Reading between the lines, it looks like our new great-grandfather was serious with a good-hearted side, from a German family. Great-grandmother was another story. She had quite the sense of humor, which my Nana says was greatly abetted by the Devil. Her humor got her through the day.

We will never know for sure if they were in love. We do know that in 1907, our new great-grandfather sent money and surprised my great-grandmother and her four children with some spending money and train tickets, to Terrace, British Columbia. The tickets came along with a letter, inviting them to travel twenty-five hundred miles to join him in a new life, in an area of the country that few people knew about and where even fewer lived.

Neither Nana nor her brothers remembered much about the trip across the country. There was too much to look forward to at the end of the line.

The Grand Trunk Pacific Railway had pushed through the Great Canadian Rockies two years before, all the way to the West Coast. The whole family was sure impressed with the natural beauty. Nana says she could hardly stop staring as the narrow valleys, rugged mountains and swift, icy rivers steered them on their journey.

Terrace was small—about 150 people. A few families and railroad workers lived in the town, with logging as the main industry. It was a tough life, but everyone was in the same situation. People just got on with their lives.

The town had a doctor, and a makeshift hospital, a school and two hotels and a few boarding houses. Rounding out the shopping experience was a large feed store, a hardware store and a small pharmacy, plus a grocery store. Two restaurants served good "home cooked meals." Sometimes the townsfolk would stop by for a piece of pie or a sandwich and a coffee. My Nana liked going in to town for a soda now and again.

There was already a pecking order in the society of Terrace. The town's newest citizens, my Nana and her family, fit right in the middle, which was fine with them. They weren't looked down on as they had been in Ontario. That made all the difference in the world.

Terrace had some rough edges. Loggers came to town on their days off from the logging camps all over the area. You could count on a brawl or two on Saturday night. It kept the town's only constable busy, and once in a while, there would be a shooting, or a knifing, when booze and tempers got the best of the loggers.

Our new great-grandfather's farm was in a fertile valley about four miles northwest of Terrace. Today, the valley guards its small farms and their overflowing gardens, and you can still feel the pioneer spirit those early settlers planted in the gardens at the turn of the century.

To the children, especially my Nana, the outdoors was a playground. Their lives were shaped by the weather: harsh, dark winters with deep snows and heavy rains. Cloudy, misty weather. Typical of the Pacific Northwest rain forest. The seasons didn't care much about the people. Spring would clear the way for better days. Then came high winds, more rain, mists, clouds and sunny periods. There was always the mud to contend with. Summers brought long bright days, with one hour flowing into another. Everyone took advantage of the light into the late evening. It wasn't unusual to hear children playing outdoors at 10 p.m. Autumns were sunny and hot, with cool nights. All through the warmer season, bugs enjoyed the human contact.

Great-grandmother wanted her children to love the outdoors, and to be hard workers.

Their new father, with his German background, taught them discipline and practical skills that they would use all their lives.

He appreciated his new wife and family. The boys tried to sort things out early on by getting into a big fight one Sunday, just before the family was to leave for church. Great-grandfather grabbed each one by the ear, marched them to the water trough, and quickly dunked their heads. When they left for church in family's wagon, the four boys enjoyed a cool ride while their clothes dried off. Getting the swelling to go down on their ears was another matter. Every morning for the next week, great-grandfather would walk around the breakfast table and grab each boy's sore ear. He'd ask if the ear was better. Before they could mumble a reply, great-grandfather would squeeze the sore spot. The boys decided then and there, it would be easier to settle any differences by holding contests. They ran, swam, climbed trees, and performed all sorts of feats of strength.

Great-grandfather said it was Nana who could out-swim, out-run, out-climb and out-smart the boys with her eyes closed. If she wanted to. He never gave her heck or squeezed her ear. He liked Nana, and was kind to her and her mother.

The one thing that Nana could do better than any person in the entire family was shoot a gun and hunt. Although Nana overdid it. She is a crack shot, and the family has enjoyed many a grouse, deer or moose brought down by her expert eye and hand.

Nana was only 15 when she met my Grandfather, William Winser Noonan, who was 27. From St. John's, Newfoundland, he was a telegrapher with the railway, hired to set up train stations along the route from the Rockies, and over the Coastal Range, west to Prince Rupert.

They decided it would be a good thing to get married, after she bailed him out of a knee-deep mud puddle one spring day by pulling him out with the end of her gun. He didn't want to get on the wrong end of her temper, or her gun.

They had a small wedding one hot September day in 1911. Just the family. That same year Grandad became a station agent and was sent to the railway junction at Pacific, a town along the Skeena River, just a few miles east of Terrace. This was where the trains heading to and fro across Canada did their northwestern turn around and high-tailed it back east.

By 1916, Telkwa's coalmine was working at top capacity, and the town was the main stop in the Bulkley Valley for livestock and feed, coal, and even people.

With the coalmine busy and the farming plentiful, Telkwa's population had risen from 250 to 850 in just over five years. (The town's size has remained pretty well the same since 1921. Telkwa incorporated in 1952. I know, because my Dad worked on the incorporation of the town when he was on council.)

Set in a wide valley, Telkwa balances at the 'V' of the Telkwa and Bulkley Rivers. It is the only town in the world where three bridges come off the same rock bluff. They are the roadway bridge, the new railway bridge and the old railway bridge. That's in the Telkwa history book, written by our family friend, Patty Phelps. (The book is for sale for $2.95 at Phelps & Saunders General Store, P.O. Box 1, Telkwa, B.C. Patty is the postmistress and she will mail you a copy of the book if you send her the money. Remember to include your address.)

The C.N.R. needed a fellow who was good-natured to run the Telkwa station. Grandad fit the bill. Bringing Nana along was both good and bad. The townsfolk weren't quite prepared for her. They liked hearing about what she was up to as long as they weren't the ones on the receiving end of her sharp wit, or her temper.

Nana and Grandad set up house at the train station in the spring of 1916. Auntie Polly and Aunt Sue were already born by then. Five years after they moved to the station, they had my Mom, Fran.

There was always a lot to do at the station. Two trains a day and passengers from all over. There was livestock around, killing time before they went to a farmer or the butcher block. The town operated a big creamery. There were cans of milk to load on the train. Grandad could lift one in each hand, right onto the train cars. He was well known for that feat. Trucks delivered coal every couple of days. Nana always had extra people for dinner.

The station wasn't built for a growing family. It only had two bedrooms and a small kitchen. Two years after my Mom was born, Nana and Grandad bought an acre that backs up to a rocky hill, right behind St. Stephen's Anglican Church. They had to give up a bit of the land to make an alley. They still live at the house behind the Anglican Church and I will bet they will until they die.

As for the 'hobbies, likes and dislikes' question in the essay, my Nana is a well-established Women's Institute member. Grandad just retired from the Canadian National Railway.

I know this about my grandparents: Number 1—Nana rules the roost. Number 2—Their hobbies are listening to Hockey Night in Canada on the radio, reading, gardening, softball, dancing, cooking, football, music, bridge, horseracing, cribbage and grouse hunting. Nana's main hobby should not be mentioned in a school essay, says my Mother. So if you want to know about it (and you do ANYWAY, Mr. Powers), I can fill you in.

At six-foot-four, Grandad is a really strong man. He has gray hair, blue eyes and a nice smile. He stays pretty quiet unless he is talking about a subject that interests him. He loves sports, and umpires softball games at the Telkwa Barbecue grounds. He can always be counted on to coach the kids and adults around town. He used to lift my cousin Martin and me onto his knees to listen to Hockey Night in Canada on CBC Radio. We were much lighter than the cans of cream he hucked around at the station.

According to all family sources, Grandad's most common phrase about Nana is, "Black is white, black is white." I don't think they argue, because I am sure that Grandad isn't that stupid. He just lets Nana have at it, and gets on with what he wants to do.

Nana is tall, almost six feet. Nana has blue eyes and mostly dark hair with a few wisps of gray by the front part. Somewhere between learning to shoot and becoming a wife and mother to three girls, Nana learned deportment and manners. Sometimes, she just forgets to use them. That's what makes her more interesting than most everybody else's Grandmothers.

Polly and Sue were born in Pacific. My Mom, Fran, was "Conceived in Telkwa and delivered by train to Prince Rupert." (That is a family joke, but I am still not sure why.) Nana was visiting the doctor when 'Wee Fran' arrived just before Christmas. Fran returned to Telkwa at three weeks old, and Nana and Grandad have lived in the house along the alley behind St. Stephen's Anglican Church ever since.

Except for when my Mom and my Dad, A.E. Mulvaney, left during WWII, the family remained living in Telkwa until a few years ago.

My Mom, Dad and I now live in Terrace and Aunt Sue lives with her family in Hazelton. But Auntie Polly lives just down the alley from Nana, behind Telkwa's John Deere Tractor shop.

Nana and Grandad's house has endured hundreds of visits from 'the pups' as Nana calls my cousins and me. The yard welcomes us with its comfortable corners and secret spots under the lilac trees. The outbuildings aid and abet us. (I know what that means, so have added it in this essay.) The barn captures history—world and family—and holds every newspaper, magazine and flyer that came through the front gate from 1923 onwards. Except the 'Watchtower magazine,' that was returned to its rightful owner every week.

The garage hosts early, mid and recent 20th Century household conveniences: stoves, fridges, sinks, tubs, showers and toilets. They are all mistrusted by Nana. Any relative or close friend getting married has to decide on one of the appliances sent to the garage and the colony of electronic and porcelain outcasts.

Besides the woodshed—which houses more wood than a sawmill—the only outbuilding that holds meaning to Nana, and is respected for its original design, is the outhouse. It has had its moments, mind you.

All of the folks in Telkwa and most of the people in Terrace and pretty well all of the kids at Skeena High have heard about Nana Noonan and her outhouse. And Nana Noonan and her Jehovah. I know a lot about my relations. I just can't tell everything I know, or I could get in trouble.

Nana knows she's getting a reputation for herself, as many of the townsfolk take great pleasure in passing on Nana Noonan stories to their friends and relatives. They tell what Nana has been up to, instead of the boring details on how many jars of strawberry jam they put up. Nana is entertaining and she is my grandmother. I am told I carry most of her strengths, and very few of her weaknesses, thank goodness.

P.S. But it's all relative. Ha Ha.

Maggie Mulvaney Grade 8, Division B.
Final Essay for Mr. Kenney Powers' Social Studies and English Class

Printed in the United States
37675LVS00002B/193-660